Shell-shocked in the Great War, Gunner Dan returned to his Tipperary village and a changed Ireland.

Nationalists had risen against the British government. In contrast to the cheers which had seen him off, he was beaten up and forced to bury his medals in the rath above his hillside house.

Described by his doctor as one of 'the forgotten generation', he considered himself lucky. Over a hundred returnees were killed.

The Gunner's zest for life, passion for nature and determination to recover his decorations enabled him to survive until normality returned.

The heady days of revolution forgotten, he becomes a village celebrity when he finally unearths his medals thirty years later. With the help of a young local boy who appreciated his sacrifices and stories.

Best-selling author Jilly Cooper calls it, 'A heroic and touching story. Brendan Lynch writes beautifully.'

About the Author

Brendan Lynch is a former racing cyclist and driver.

Old enough to have met Bertrand Russell, Brendan Behan, and James Baldwin, he served a month in Brixton prison for his 1960s CND anti-war activities.

As a journalist, he contributed to mainstream Irish media, as well as to *The Observer, Times* and *European*. He was a consultant for *The Encyclopaedia of Ireland*.

His books include three on literary and Bohemian Dublin and the definitive account of Alcock and Brown's first nonstop Atlantic flight. An award-winning motorsport history and the equally racy *Princess of the Orient* on his misadventures in South East Asia.

The Old Gunner and His Medals

Brendan Lynch

Mountjoy Publishing

Published by
Mountjoy Publishing
5 Mid Mountjoy Street
Dublin 7
www.brendanlynch.ie

A catalogue record of this book is available
from the British Library.

ISBN 978-0-9513668-3-7

Printed in Spain by GraphyCems

Contents

Jane had shiny black hair and was
ready for any mischief (p. 91)

Since independence, the Great War is not taught in Irish schools. Consequently, few now know about the soldiers' sacrifices, or the killing of so many after they returned. The forgotten generation.
– *Doctor J. C. Murphy.*

Of all evils of war, the greatest is the purely spiritual evil: the hatred, the injustice, the repudiation of truth, the artificial conflict.
– *Bertrand Russell.*

Dedication

To the Gunner and his comrades
who suffered at home, as well as
at Mons and Ypres.

1.

A Shadow Swept Across the Flowerbeds

He caught a familiar, mustier odour

'Down, Dan! Down! This one's for us,' Liverpool Pat pushed.

Gunner Dan slid to the bottom of the trench. He pulled the helmet tighter over his head and held his breath. The shell tore into the ramp above them. The ground shook, a fellow-soldier screamed. Stones, shrapnel and clay rained down. Another near-miss. How much longer could he stand this? 'The war will be over be Christmas, me arse,' he spat out the earth.

The Gunner woke, sweating and shaking. Another bloody nightmare. Wouldn't you think that

1

after three decades they'd have exhausted themselves? But how much better in the morning than during the night. And how much safer than the real thing. The sun rippled on the wall opposite his bed. A blackbird led the dawn chorus. Was there any more joyous sound on earth? How good to be back in his own little village after the mayhem of Mons and Ypres. How lucky to be in one piece, while so many mates had perished.

He stirred the embers of the fire, placed the last of his sticks on top and hung the saucepan of oats overhead to boil. He poured water from the bucket into a white enamel basin, splashed his face and congratulated himself on having shaved yesterday. Strange how simple tasks took longer as one aged. He didn't neglect the morning ritual of straightening the Angelus picture. More memories.

Pulling up his patched tweed trousers, he buttoned his once-red shirt and limped outside to check the weather. Half seven, the sparrows were foraging already, the sun was creeping over Carroll's hurling field. Low-lying mists surrendered to its warmth, it lit up the green fields all the way to the heights of Keeper Hill. The panorama was his morning tonic. Such space after the confinement of cordite-laden trenches. Heaven after hell, he reflected, as he gulped in the clean air.

As he did every day, the Gunner turned towards the furze-crowned hillock above his house, raised his right hand and saluted. The Ireland he'd returned to in 1918 was no heaven. No longer the tranquil country of his dug-out dreams. Nationalists had risen against the British government. After all they'd already endured, many of his comrades were killed. Fearful of extremists, he'd buried his war medals inside the hill rath. His secret for so long, no one in Toomevara knew. 'Youse may get me, but you'll never lay hands on me decorations,' he'd determined.

The medals were all he had to show for his years at the Front. He missed them almost every day. Unsure after so many years of the exact hiding place, he'd looked for them many times without success. Were they still there, could they really have survived thirty winters underground? But, he wouldn't give up hope. This week, he'd start his final search. The thought cheered him.

'Don't worry, Salvo,' he greeted a robin who wobbled beside the doorway. 'You'll have your crumbs after I do me bit of shopping. We'll have you better in no time.'

He hastened inside, stirred the steaming porridge and emptied it into a large green bowl. He added a spoon of sugar from a frayed paper bag and poured in the can of milk he'd bought last

3

night at Delaney's. Oats had been his breakfast for over sixty year, was there any better way to start the day?

After washing the bowl, he sat on the stone beside the door and lit his pipe. FrenchShea's pub had absorbed most of his pension, but he'd ensured enough baccy to last until next payday. Monday, the start of a new week. The best day to prepare his big quest. With a new spade and a crowbar promised by neighbour Bill O'Meara, he would have the most efficient tools. The years were catching up. Whatever happened, he wouldn't rest until he unearthed his decorations. It would be great if he could get someone to help, even if it meant finally sharing his secret. He thought of the only person in the village who had shown interest in his war adventures. Maybe the boy could join him, now that it was school holidays?

His tobacco finished, the Gunner tapped the pipe against the stone and slid it into his trousers pocket. Collecting his cap, he went down the slope and out through a gap in the hedge. He headed up to the village for his bread and the latest news. Insects buzzed, blue tits piped, robins chirped from every bush. 'A great day to be alive, I wish I'd your energy,' he doffed his cap.

4

Waking in his riverside house, the boy had welcomed the same encouraging sun. It reminded him of the poem Mrs Hogan had taught him in second class:

> I remember, I remember,
> The house where I was born,
> The little window where the sun
> Came peeping in at morn;
> He never came a wink too soon,
> Nor brought too long a day...

What a lovely June morning. And all the more exciting because it was the start of school holidays. Freedom! A whole week with nothing to do. And, imagine, for the following two months, until he graduated to long trousers and joined the big boys in secondary school. Monday blossomed with possibilities.

He could hear the water splashing out from under the bridge and imagine its sparkle as it danced down the ledge he had christened Niagara. Like music, the first and last sound he heard each day. It might be only one foot deep, but the river was a magical place. He could play and dream there as if in another world. Catching minnows, studying the swirling weeds and the wagtails darting from rock to mossy rock. Sometimes, he collected stones and made his own waterfall.

But how could he persuade his mother to allow him down there today? She had kept him indoors yesterday after he had slipped and soaked his trousers. If the river was out of bounds, maybe she would let him play draughts after supper with saddler Gordon Birch? Or go and save the hay with Johnny Kennedy? Few pleasures matched that of riding back into the village with the sweet-smelling hay. His legs dangling from the end of the sloping cart as he plucked stray stems from his hair.

Their house was in the centre the village. After breakfast, he stood in the broad-windowed porch which local character, the old Gunner, had christened the observation post. Blue lupins and yellow wallflowers enlivened the front flowerbeds. Looking across the flowers and the white railings, he could see everything in the main street of ten shops and five pubs. Postman Jim O'Rourke doing his rounds, farmers trotting to the creamery with laden milk churns. Father Kenny on his morning constitutional, Johnny Armstrong staggering home with two buckets of water from the pump for his large family. Big Jim O'Meara coming out to check the weather. And the lucky passengers in the green bus which swept around the barracks at ten o'clock and stopped at Jim's Bridge House, before resuming its long journey from Limerick to Dublin.

He went out and sat on the front garden's wrought-iron bench, his mother's summer reading place. Not a cloud in the sky, the sun climbed higher over Boland's mill. Closing his eyes, he listened to the water and savoured the scent of the wallflowers. He thought of the children in his Arthur Ransome library book, embarking on another Lake District exploration. How he wished he could adventure with them. He sensed a shadow sweeping across the flowerbeds and caught a familiar, mustier odour. He opened his eyes. It was someone who also animated their village. Toome's only voyager, none other than the Gunner himself.

The Gunner lived alone underneath the fairy rath on the Silvermines road. Often shouting in the street at night, many villagers said that he was mad. And stupid, as he had lost his war medals. The children laughed at him and imitated his slouch. 'Dan's cracked, as well as not being able to read or write. And you can tell he's coming a mile away by the stink of his clothes.'

'Dan was shell-shocked in the Great War and that smell is the tobacco in his clay pipe,' he protested. He wondered how classmates could be so cruel to a man who had suffered so much.

Of medium height, his battered grey cap at an angle, the Gunner was wearing a torn red shirt and the trousers of the brown suit which teacher Tom MacDonald had passed on to him years before. His ruddy angular face was as lively as usual, but the check shirt seemed too large for him. 'The years and his travails are catching up, amazing he has survived so far,' Doctor Murphy had told his father one evening.

His mother came out. 'Good morning, Dan, a lovely day, thank God. How is the health?'

The Gunner pushed the cap back over his greying hair and rocked across the railings. '*Suas, sios*, up and down, as the scholar said. The hip's playing up, the doc wants to do a bit more poking around. But, you're right. 'Tis a day to be out and about, and not fretting about health or the price of eggs in China. You should sit down there with one of your books and give the housework a miss. And if that young son of yours wants to play for a couple of hours above me house, he's very welcome.'

'Trust you for the constructive word, Dan,' his mother opened the railings gate. 'But you would need the patience of Job to cope with this fellow, he is always getting into mischief. He celebrated his twelfth birthday on Saturday by falling off the apple tree. Only yesterday, he came home dripping wet after slipping on the weeds under the bridge. Would you watch him and take no nonsense? Maybe, he could occupy himself searching for that treasure everyone talks about – though I doubt if there is anything buried up there?'

'There might be something, if a person knew where to look,' the Gunner winked at him. 'I'll keep an eye on him, mam, you needn't worry. Maybe even join in the digging and make him a nice cup of tay afterwards.'

Why had the Gunner winked? Did he know something no one else did? Was there really treasure in the rath?

'Rest yourself on the seat for a minute, Dan,' his mother invited. 'I'll get a snack for your tea.'

'*Nice* biscuits, *trés bon*, one of me favourites after fig-rolls. Like your lovely lavender, they remind me of France. But 'twas far from Nice I was in 1914, mam. I hear the sun always shines there, even in winter.'

'You are the only one in the village who can speak French, Dan,' his mother complimented.

'Sure, wasn't I at the best academies of all, the Somme and the Marne?'

'A long way from Toome and from the Riviera,' her tone softened.

9

'I wish it had been the south of France. While me mates and I were dodging bombs and bullets, the rich folk down there were dipping their toes in the warm Mediterranean.'

'I would like to see it myself too,' his mother looked down the street. 'But, if this fellow and yourself find anything this morning, maybe we will all go south and have sunshine every day?'

His mother was strict, it was nice to hear her joking. And so early in the morning. For a change, she had not given out to the Gunner about his drinking. There was a lot to be said for the sun. And for the Gunner. According to his father, he always made people forget their problems. 'Be a good boy for Dan. Make sure you are back by half one for lunch,' his mother closed the gate behind them.

The Gunner was more interesting than most villagers, who only discussed the weather and politics. He regularly told stories and even recited poetry:

> What is this life, if full of care,
> We have no time to stand and stare.
> No time to see, when woods we pass,
> Where squirrels hide their nuts in grass.

He could remember Toomevara in the old days before Dick Casey installed a petrol pump outside his cycle shop for the new motor cars. When there was a weekly market and when everyone walked or cycled to the cross-roads dances or to Nenagh or neighbouring Moneygall for hurling matches. He had recently related some of his war experiences to the boy's parents. 'France and Belgium, you couldn't believe the devastation. Houses and towns reduced to rubble, bodies everywhere. 'Twas like the end of the world.

'And when I finally got back, I didn't find the quiet I'd dreamt of. Only more fighting. The Somme might have been safer, at least there you knew who your enemies were. After all they'd already endured, many of me poor comrades were shot dead. Two young policemen were killed on their way home from the chapel up there – unarmed men, keeping the peace like yourself, Sergeant. In the history books, they're now villains and their killers heroes. Is it me that's mixed up or the world?'

His mother had made no comment. As religious as she was nationalistic, she had reminded 'You won't forget the Mission, Dan? The Passionists are back next month.'

"We're all pilgrims, mam, but I think those fellas do more to put people off than to convert them. Shouting from the altar, their cassocks fly-

11

ing in the air. All their talk about an eternity of fire and brimstone, it's enough to test a saint. Surely, religion shouldn't be about frightening people? I think the only ones who benefit are the traders outside the church wall. They do a roaring trade in insurance policies - beads, scapulars, holy pictures. Maybe they're all in cahoots?'

'Dan, you are an awful pagan, I will pray for you this evening.'

'This evening might be too late,' the Gunner had tilted his cap.

The boy's father was the village Garda sergeant. Every morning after half-past eight Mass, he walked the hundred yards to the barracks at the end of the village, his uniform buttons and belt buckle gleaming. He was proud that his father was in charge of the Garda station. But, as his mother often insisted 'It is no easy job, laying down the law to neighbours who would prefer to bicker and grab land that does not belong to them.'

'For men may come and men may go, But I go on forever,' the Gunner looked down at the water, as they retraced his father's path across the bridge.

The boy sometimes dreamt of following the river all the way to the Shannon and its final home in the big Atlantic. Maybe, some of its water washed New York, where his aunts and uncles now lived? Perhaps, he could travel there one day? Meantime, he could adventure with the Gunner's stories. Apart from those who went to work in England, no one else in their village had travelled, not even his teachers, Mrs Hogan and Tom MacDonald. Perhaps villagers who made fun of the Gunner were jealous that he had been abroad, even if to the war?

They passed Big Jim O'Meara's pub and Ciss MacDonald's pharmacy. Across the street, Ger Devaney and Jim Hickey were removing forms from the hall. 'You were in mighty voice last Friday,' Ger shouted. 'You had everyone in FrenchShea's singing your favourite, "Tipperary".'

'Three days in the fields with Dick Hassett and it all went in one evening,' the Gunner waved his arms.

'You were right, Dan,' Jim hoisted another seat. 'You can't take it with you.'

They reached Mrs Kelly's bakery, from which the aroma of newly baked bread wafted down the street every morning. A cheering alarm call, like Billy Delaney's whistling, as his cows slith-ered home to be milked. The Gunner went in and bought a small white loaf. The boy's mother sometimes got bread there, but she did not like the Kellys. Their family had opposed her hero, de Valera in the Civil War.

As they reached Mrs McLoughney's shop opposite the barracks, the Gunner rummaged in his pockets. 'There's a penny. Go in and buy a toisin of bullseyes for the two of us. Not the best for the teeth – but I won't tell your mother, if you don't.'

They turned down the curve of the Silvermines road. Two hundred yards ahead of them, the yellow furze above the Gunner's house reflected the morning sun. Visible from a mile away, the hilltop display cheered everyone who saw it.

'A great year for the birds,' Dan looked up, as swallows swooped ahead of them and sparrows swayed on the telegraph lines. Climbing ivy had transformed the poles into trees, wild roses pushed through the ripening blackberries. There should be lots of jam this autumn. 'Doesn't the woodbine smell lovely, Dan?' he buried his nose in a creamy blossom.

The Gunner shook his head 'You know I can't smell any bloody thing since the war gaz and shells.'

'Sorry, Dan,' he dug his fingernails into the palms of his hands.

They went through the hedge into the Gunner's field. Half way up the slope, his single-storey home stood out against the surrounding

14

greenery. Some slates were missing, the remains of a lace curtain fluttered through a hole in the bottom righthand window. Bordered by red wildflowers and glinting in the sun, a granite slab made a convenient doorside bench. A clump of orange wallflowers and white foxgloves enlivened the flagstone, where a robin huddled with drooping wings.

'Salvo, me sentry,' Dan lifted the latch. 'I called him after a little Italian mate who was always singing. As bad on the pins as meself, he flopped down here a week ago with a mangled right leg. I've been feeding him since, you've got to be fighting fit to survive in the wild. Come in for a minute while I get his crumbs and some water for his saucer.'

Dust danced in the light rays, an old herringbone overcoat swung from its hook behind the faded green door. Lit by three small windows and a skylight, the boy had to accustom himself to the gloom. The stone house was about the size of two rooms in his own home. It smelled of dirty socks, lucky the other children were not with him. 'Not as grand as your riverside mansion,' the Gunner spilled some water, as he poured from a small bucket.

The floor's red tiles were well worn, it was a long time since the walls had been whitewashed.

An enamel basin and a small cracked mirror rested on an oak stand under the doorside window. Frayed dark blankets covered a single metal bed at the end of the house. A pine dresser against the rear wall boasted some odd plates, cups and cutlery. The Gunner had no kettle. He boiled water from the nearby well in one of the two saucepans which rested on the smoke-blackened hob. A pair of wooden chairs flanked the fireplace opposite the door. Dripping oil, a grey tin lamp and a saucer with a half-used white candle rested on a shelf to the left. A dark-framed painting with broken glass hung at an angle above them.

'The Angelus, we have that at home. Would you like me to get new glass for yours?' he asked Dan.

'Millet, wasn't he a great man with the paint brush, the way he could catch a moment? I'll tell you a story about this, an image that will stay forever in me mind,' the Gunner took down the picture.

'Near the end of the war, a few of us sheltered one rainy morning in a cottage in northern France. The woman of the house welcomed us with coffee underneath that very picture. We were hardly a quarter of a mile down the road, when the shells started. We looked around. The roof was gone from the home, bits of furniture were scattered everywhere. We raced back. The woman and her husband were dead beside the fireplace. Their boy of about your age had been blown into the bedroom, the picture smashed beside him. I thought the only way I could repay them for their kindness was to look after it for them. Thanks for the offer, but I'll keep it exactly as I found it.'

An object that had endured the war, like the Gunner, he could not believe it. 'No clock, how do you tell the time?' he followed Dan out into the light.

The Gunner pointed to the sun. 'There's me timepiece. Good enough for Crusoe and Saint Patrick, good enough for me. Never wrong, never needs to be wound up.'

Skirting the little back garden with its rose tree, potato patch and well-ventilated wooden privy, they climbed up towards the rath. He wondered if the Gunner was frightened when the winter winds blasted around the slope at night. 'Only sometimes. The hill protects me from the worst of the storms and, facing south, I've the best views and more sun than anyone in the village.'

'Was that place really a fairy rath?' he followed Dan along the well-beaten track.

'You're always talking about the little people and buried gold,' the Gunner looked down at him. 'You're reading too much of those County Council library books. But maybe one day, with a bit of luck, we'll dig up something worthwhile.'

Was the Gunner joking? Was he cracked, like villagers said? Could there really be treasure up there?

2.

The Gunner's Secret

*'No one else must know for the time being,
not even your parents.'*

'I am the blaze on every hill,' the Gunner squeezed ahead of him through the sweet-smelling furze. 'Now, I need a few twigs to get me own fire going again.'

He placed a fallen bough under his boot. A pair of pigeons flapped their wings as it snapped in two. 'It will take ten minutes to boil the water. You stay here and play. If you find anything, give me a shout. Mind those hawthorns, as prickly as the furze. If you get cut, herself will be after me.'

The Gunner gathered up the branches. 'Did you know that the hawthorn's a sacred tree, the

19

gateway to the world of the Sidhe? Its blossoms announce the arrival of Spring, a special time for them. That furze around us makes the best yellow dye and flavoured whiskey in the ould times. It was the favourite of Lugh, the Celtic god of light, after whom the harvest feast of Lughnasadh is called. He was one of the ancient Tuatha De Danann tribe, who may have lived on this very hill. But, I'll tell you more when you come down. We'll enjoy your biscuits outside the door and admire the view.'

The boy was looking forward to hearing the rest of the Gunner's story. But, how did he know so much, when he had not even finished school? 'He's a walking encyclopaydya,' odd-job man Paddy Dwyer had told his mother.

He could not resist climbing the old oak, the tallest tree and best vantage point in the village. Insects hummed unseen as he edged out along a branch and pushed aside the leaves. Toomevara stretched out below him, from the priests' house on the left to the Protestant church at the other end. It all looked so remote from where he was hidden. But how safe it seemed compared to night-time, when he raced from one shop-window light to another, fearful of the shadows in between. Climbing was exhilarating, like opening a new window on the world. He wished the

Gunner could climb but his hip had been damaged in the fighting. His mother said it was a miracle he could walk at all.

When he had seen enough of the village, he climbed down. Relishing a sweet red clover, he slowly traversed the rath. Roots and shrubs everywhere but, apart from a pile of stones, he saw no place where there might be buried treasure. Stepping sideways, he exited through the bushes, stretched out on the soft grass and started to roll down the hill. Over and over he went. His head started spinning. He knew he would be unable to stop, unless he sat up. Even then, it took him several more turns before he finally slowed. Speed was scary but it was also exciting, no wonder he loved his bike. He might try a few more tumbles later.

'Tay-time,' the Gunner shouted. 'If herself sees you covered in grass, we'll all be in the dog-house. Wear a dark shirt next time. Sit down there on me stone and I'll bring you the nicest cuppa you ever tasted.'

The once-blue mugs were chipped but, after his exercise, he was too thirsty to care. In front of them, the green fields stretched across the plain to the hills overlooking their village. Keeper's peak seemed so distant. 'A good sign, like the swallows flying high,' the Gunner pointed. 'For if it looks close, it's time to be heading home, rain's on the way. We could learn a lot from our feathered friends.'

The Gunner paused his mug. 'Do you know, there were times when I thought I'd never enjoy that view or climb Keeper or the Devil's Bit again. Instead of this lovely grass, I slithered in mud and wondered if I'd live another day. As you're the only youngster in the village who's asked me about it, I'll tell you more when I'm in the humour.'

'Dan, why do they say there's treasure buried up there?'

'Most villagers don't know it, but that rath was probably the first settlement in Toome. It and all the others around Ireland were once the homes of the Tuatha De Danann. They built earthbanks around the hilltops to defend themselves and their animals. Then invaders arrived and the De Danann fled underground with all their goods and treasure. Many people claim to have heard their music and seen lights at night coming from the rath. With all the drinking that goes on around here, I'm not surprised. They also say there's gold buried there.'

'Do you believe in the treasure stories?' he drained his tea.

'I can't say I do and I can't say I don't. Many yarns are handed down about the olden times.

Some must be true, but a lot were embroidered over the years. I don't believe in anything people tell me anymore. Since the war, I now only believe in things I can see for meself. But, maybe one day soon I might be able to tell you about something hidden up there – as long as you promise to keep it a secret. I'm going to start looking for it soon. But no one else must know for the time being, not even your parents. Only you and me.'

Buried treasure in the rath after all? He was startled by the revelation. And the Gunner and he were the only two people who knew. He would love to be involved in the search, what an adventure that would be. Maybe, Dan would invite him to help? Or had he been only joking? But he had never heard him exaggerate or say anything he did not mean. His attitude suggested he knew something other villagers did not. It would be hard work keeping the knowledge to himself, his first big secret. But he must not let down the Gunner. 'I will not tell anyone, not even my father and mother,' he shook Dan's calloused hand.

'Your mother! We'd better get you home on time – or I'll never be able to tell you about me new campaign.'

'If I am there a few minutes early, she will let me come back again. Maybe on Thursday and maybe then you can tell me more?'

'You're the only lad I'd trust in the village, we'll do that – but make sure not a whisper to anyone.'

He brushed the grass off his shirt and trousers, as they walked up to the village. His mother was reading on the garden seat.

'Well, Dan,' she put down her book. 'Only a quarter past. You said you would bring him home in time and you have.'

'He was a good lad, we'd a great chat. He can come down again any time. We didn't do any treasure hunting, maybe next time.'

'We will see how he behaves himself meantime. He is a bit lazy, the exercise would do him no harm. Now, here is something for looking after him. And do not spend it in Harty's or FrenchShea's on the way home.'

She handed the Gunner a shilling and they both watched him safely past both pubs. Dick Hassett's donkey and cart with an empty milk churn were parked outside Harty's, a bicycle leaned against the wall. His mother went inside to make the lunch. The donkey hee-hawed loudly, but not enough to deter the Gunner. His cap reappeared around the corner a few seconds later and disappeared through the pub door.

'Dan is more reliable than most in the village, despite his problems,' his mother served up his lunchtime soup. 'If you are a good boy, I might let you see him again in a few days. Did he give you one of his lectures?'

The Gunner had a reputation for being able to discuss any subject from nature to world affairs. 'A mighty explainer, but do not stop unless you have a morning to spare,' insisted Molly Barney, no mean talker herself.

The boy was sorry that the Gunner could not read properly. One of his own biggest treats was the fortnightly Council library with its Robert Louis Stevenson, Patricia Lynch and other riches. 'Books are like a key to the world,' his mother had been right.

'Why did you not finish school, Dan?' he had once enquired.

'Little choice, I'd to work and help me parents, I got three times more in the army than I could in the fields. I'm sorry when Bill O'Meara shows me books I cannot read. But, maybe I've learned more from the school of hard knocks than many have from their studying. Most only use their book knowledge to make money. Then they go around with their heads in the air and miss the wonder of everything. Dead notes in their wallets and the birds celebrating all around them. And the more they have, the more worried they are. I didn't need books to learn that it's giving that makes people happiest, not taking, nor spondulix. It reminds me of a poem Bill once recited for me:

> The world is too much with us; late and soon,
> Getting and spending, we lay waste our
>   powers;—
> Little we see in nature that is ours;
> We have given our hearts away, a sordid boon!

That evening, the boy's father removed the glass bowl of their pedestal lamp and lit the oil wick. How ornate it was compared to the Gunner's leaking tin. Sitting under the light, the boy trawled through *Treasure Island* and other books on buried booty. 'X marks the spot.' Stirring tales with charts and diagrams but offering little guidance to a modern treasure-hunter. The Gunner had an advantage over those earlier searchers. The pirates had to search vast areas, the rath covered only a small space. Any cache might prove hard to find but, with time and planning, he felt it could be done.

But what was it and why had Dan seemed so sure? He thought about the rath, where he had often played cowboys and Indians with other children. And fantasised about hidden gold, without knowing that there might have been something there after all. He retrieved a school jotter and started to draw his own chart of the rath. A rough sketch of everything he could remember there. From the rim of trees and the gaps in the earth-bank to the centre bushes and the pile of stones.

'What on earth is this?' his mother picked up the page.

'My treasure map of the rath, just like Robert Louis Stevenson drew.'

'And everyone thinks the poor Gunner is the daftest the village.'

'Can I go down again and play on the hill?' he twisted his pencil.

'Maybe on Thursday, it would be better than getting wet in the river. The Gunner must be lonely there by himself, it would be a bit of company for him too. It was a pity that nice Grenanstown girl he knew years ago went off to England.'

His mother was right about Dan's need for company. He had heard him tell Bill O'Meara one evening 'The pub's the only place if you're under the weather. A bit of chat and you soon forget your troubles. Everyone says the jar's bad for you. The opposite's true. If people relaxed over a cruiskeen, they'd get to know each other better. There would be more fun, less misunderstanding. When I'm taoiseach, I'll make drinking compulsory.'

The Gunner was not lonely in Harty's. Dick Hassett and Paddy Carthy were there after delivering their milk to the creamery. Paring a new tobacco plug with his penknife, the Gunner's pipe smoke rose to the snug ceiling. It was like the mighty nights in the *estaminets*, the French she-beens. He would never forget the camaraderie, as he and his mates enjoyed rare breaks behind the lines around the open stoves. Not a shell nor an officer in sight, the best omelettes he had ever tasted, wine and beer fuelling their stories and shanties. The memories spurred him into song:

> 'The Kaiser knows each Munster, be the
>   Shamrock on his cap,
> And the famous Bengal Tiger, ever ready
>   for a scrap.
> With all his big battalions, Prussian guards
>   and grenadiers,
> He feared to face the bayonets of the
>   Munster Fusiliers.'

'Dan, the last of the fearless Fusiliers, you'd lift a bad wake, but how the hell did you survive that war?' Dick cradled his pint.

'Two hundred thousand of us left from here to fight,' the Gunner unclamped his pipe.

'Up to a quarter were killed, including fifteen hundred from Tipp. Wasn't I the lucky one to escape? Me best friend in the trenches was Liverpool Pat.

' "Do as I do, go with the flow," he helped me recover from me first bombardment.

' "Duck and dive and you'll survive." 'We both did and that's been me motto ever since.'

'Well done, Dan, you've seen and done more than all the rest of us put together. You might duck and dive but no better man to work, I hope you'll be free later for the beet-thinning. I'd better go now before that bloody ass of mine deafens the entire village.'

His shilling spent and Dick's praise ringing in his ears, the Gunner headed home in the sun. As he walked, he marvelled at the greenery and bird-song, and the pleasure of a pint and good company. Peace was a precious gift. His was a great country to be in at summertime. But, going up the slope to his house, he stopped with a start. He recalled the fearful night three decades earlier, when he'd buried his decorations. Ireland hadn't been such a wonderful country then. Even veterans' families were not safe. Below in Silvermines, a soldier's 70-year-old father, George Sheehan, had been shot dead.

Where was the best place to hide them? The rath of course, only a few yards away. And if anyone went searching, there was enough space and thorny bushes to keep them busy for years. The medals were part of his life, his proudest possessions. He'd have to leave them until things calmed down, would he ever see them again?

'Time cures everything,' he lifted up each one. 'I'll wear you again, no matter how long we're parted.'

As he started packing the medals, he could see the faces of fellow-soldiers who hadn't survived to hold their own awards. His were all he had to show for four fearful years. Was it all a bad dream? The Queen Mary brass box in which he kept his decorations and three sovereigns from London suddenly looked fragile. How long would it last in the ground? The ribbons would surely lose their blue and orange colours but wouldn't that be a small price to pay if everything was saved? He coated each medal with petroleum jelly, then wound brown paper around them to protect the ribbons. He put the sovereigns on top. How many pints he could buy with those.

He laid them all in a tobacco pouch which fitted neatly inside the hinged box. Covering it with patches from his army cape, he deposited the box in a larger biscuit tin. He closed the lid and wrapped several layers of red oil tablecloth around that. He finally secured the package, now grown to a foot square, with binding twine. 'Job done,' he put on his cap. 'That should keep you snug and dry 'til I collect you again.'

He went to the front door, looked down the slope, then back to the silent village. Not a soul in sight. The moon was full, he knew he could be observed if there was anyone around. But, without the same moon, he wouldn't be able to see properly when burying the medals. He crept to the back of the house and collected his battered spade. He started up the slope, trampling the sleeping daisies. The spade tight against his body, he looked around regularly. Still no sight of anyone. And no sound but the howling of a dog further down the road, which was echoed by another in the distance. Was there anything as lonesome as the cry of a dog in the middle of the night?

Reaching the rath, he climbed over the earth ramp and through the furze. Where would make the best hiding place? Under the oak? That would be too obvious a site, if anyone came looking. Beside one of the smaller trees or bushes? He looked at the heap of red rocks. Another likely place for searchers to investigate. To his left, a young hawthorn had started to grow. A less conspicuous spot, he would bury his treasure between the two of them. The sacred hawthorn would watch over his hard-earned medals. As he started digging, he was startled by a rustling in the bushes. Was someone concealed there? He felt as vulnerable as he had been during the war. He looked around, there was no one. Probably a rat or bird he'd disturbed.

The moon vanished momentarily, he sensed a movement behind him. But it was only a branch waving gently in the night breeze. Now, he knew how easy it was for people to imagine ghosts and apparitions. He worked quickly, how well he'd learned to dig at the Front. Making as little noise as possible, he moved the many small stones one by one. A heap of earth grew in front of him. He laid the stones in a separate pile, they would come in handy for lining the hideaway. After twenty minutes, he was down almost two feet. The hole was over one foot square, perfect size for the biscuit tin. 'That will do nicely,' he straightened his back and laid down the spade.

Skirting the furze, he surveyed the countryside beneath him. No movement of either animal or fellow- human, how peaceful it all seemed. But he knew that, like in the war, all was never as it appeared to be. Down there, were people who might kill him. He went inside and collected his parcel. From the shadow of the door, he checked his surroundings again. No sounds, no voices. He was all alone in the moonlight.

He started up the slope, holding the package in front of him. He was soon back inside the rath. It was like a burial, as he lowered the package and anchored it down with a larger stone. How many of those he had witnessed. A soldier's helmet crowning the fresh mound, as comrades looked at each other and wondered who'd be next. He fed in the protective stones and first spadefuls of earth. The package soon disappeared from view. When would he see it again? Standing up, he wondered if the freshly disturbed clay could be easily spotted. Ignoring the scratches, he peeled some clods of earth from under the furze and patted these down on the hole. Soon, it was undistinguishable from the surrounding floor.

He looked to his left to doublecheck that no one had seen him. As he turned back, he got his biggest fright. Someone was moving beside him. Well, they would have to fight as hard as he had for his decorations. He tightened his grip on the spade and looked slowly to his right. It took him a few seconds to realise it was only his moon shadow on the pile of rocks. He recovered his breath. The same heap would provide a reliable marker when he returned. The hole was deep. The covering should keep out the damp, he'd done the best he could. He put the spade on his shoulder as if it were his war rifle. 'The Gunner always keeps his promises, I'll be back,' he saluted.

Fatigued but relieved, he scrambled down the slope. He made one last scan of his surroundings before parking the spade and going indoors. Rummaging behind the jug, he found his tobacco and matches and was soon puffing away on the stone outside his door. All the fields were laid out under the moon, its sheen lit up the land as far as Keeper. 'Now the musketeers can go and fuck themselves,' he wiped his bleeding hands. 'They won't get me medals. But how long before they come looking for me?'

3.

The Gunner Has Visitors

'I wasn't as cracked as they thought I was.'

The Gunner knocked after lunch on Thursday. 'He has been well behaved for a change, Dan,' the boy's mother answered the door. 'He can stay all afternoon if that is all right with you. And here is something you might enjoy, a corner of apple tart straight out of the oven.'

'You could put Kelly's out of business, mam, your apple and cloves are the talk of the village,' the Gunner tipped his cap. 'He'll be back at six, you needn't worry. And we'll enjoy the apple tart with our tay, as we watch the sun cruise across the hills.'

Climbing to the Gunner's house, the boy wondered if this would be the day he would learn more about the treasure. He did not have to wait for long.

'I promised I'd tell you about what's buried up there. But, as I said, it must be our secret for now. Sit down there on the stone and make yourself comfortable. It's a story best told over a cuppa, we'll eat that lovely cake while it's warm,' the Gunner went inside to boil the water.

He emerged with two slices of apple tart. 'And don't forget, you're the first person in the village to hear me story. Everything I tell you must be among just the two of us for the time being. For thirty year, I've had to keep it to meself. It's a great relief to finally get it off me chest.'

'No one but us will know, Dan,' he was impatient to hear the Gunner's big confidence.

'It's a long story, I'll tell you only part of it. People say I lost me medals. I never did, but I couldn't tell anyone that. When the war finished, I came back with me head high. Brass bands when we left, I thought 'twould be the same again, I'd be a village hero. But the place had become as deadly as the Western Front. John Redmond had secured Home Rule after years of campaigning. I'd supported him, who wants to be ruled be another country?' the Gunner sipped.

'But hotheads who wouldn't wait until after the war to see it implemented rose up against the government. They destroyed the lovely country I knew. The gun became law, intimidation the fashion. People who'd cheered me off, now crossed to the other side of the street. Afraid to be seen talking to me, they'd every excuse under the sun. "Sorry, Dan, I'm late for the bus," or "Billy Delany's waiting for me below on the farm."

'It was a hard lesson on how easily people could be led hither or thither, like chaff on a windy day. I'd good reason to be afraid. There were fellas here who wanted to shoot me. But, the shelling that had affected me so badly also saved me life. Some villagers felt sorry for me, the parish priest spoke to the wild men, I was saved. But, it was a scary experience. I felt anything could still happen, I lay awake many nights.

'And sure enough, they arrived one evening. I'd been expecting their visit for some time. If they couldn't get me, they'd get me decorations. They burst in the door, four of them, led be Jack Hourican.

' "You know why we're here," he jostled me inside.'

' "You want to hear of me adventures at the Front?"

'There was no ducking and diving with those boyos.'

37

' "You should have been at home, fighting for Ireland."

' "The army was the only job I could get when I left school."

' "The British army, the traitor's army, you should be shot for betraying your country."

' "This is my country too, I didn't betray anyone. I went off with the church's blessing to save Catholic Belgium and France from the Germans. It took the best years of me life, I was lucky not to be buried alive in the trenches several times."

' "You're lucky to have escaped here as well. If it wasn't for the PP you'd be at the bottom of a boghole now."

'He pushed me down on the floor and gave me a kick for good measure. There was hatred in his blue eyes, the likes of which I'd never seen in a human being before. Not even during the war. Two of the men just looked on, they'd been among the crowd who'd waved me off a few year before.

' "That's enough, Jack," one of the gang put a hand on his shoulder. "Dan's not the same man we all knew when we were growing up. He's been through enough. We're only here for the medals. Let's get them and go."

'So, as I feared, that's what they were after, me poor decorations.

' "I paid a high price for those, you shouldn't take them from me."

' "You'll pay a damn sight more if you don't get them – now. Where are they?" Jack pushed the other man aside.

' "Try the red jug," one of the men who'd been at school with me pointed to the dresser.

'Jack swept it off the shelf, it broke in a hundred pieces on the floor. Me only jug. He tore open the envelope which had been inside.

' "The War Medal and the Victory Medal. Victory my arse. We did what the Kaiser couldn't, we made those bastards run," he threw the medals down on the table.

'He took a hammer from beside the fireplace and beat the Victory Medal until it wasn't round anymore.'

' "The first square medal," me schoolmate laughed, as its ring suspender flew off.

'Jack held up the decorations. "Tatty ribbons and bits of tin, that's what you risked your life and betrayed your country for. You're madder than we thought. But we'll keep them both, they could come in useful," he put the envelope in his pocket.

' "We got what we came for, let's leave," the quieter man took his arm again.

'The big one had the last word.'

' "Not a whisper to anyone about us calling," he shook me until I fell over a chair and landed on me bad leg again.

' "Neither the police, the PP, nor the neighbours. Or we'll be back and even the Bishop won't save you this time."

'Jack was one of the gang who killed those policemen on the square.'

Jack Hourican, who had visited their house, a murderer. The boy could not believe it. He was equally shocked that, apart from the Gunner, no one in the village had ever mentioned the killings. Instead of trying to make amends, they had covered them up.

'When they'd gone, I sat down on the floor to compose meself. I'm not afraid to tell you, I cried. That men could be so vicious - and towards a neighbour who'd never done them any harm. 'Twould make you ashamed to be a human being. Ashamed to be Irish. And me grandmother's lovely jug smashed to smithereens. As I swept up the pieces and straightened the chairs, I wondered if the whole world had gone mad. That men could prefer fighting to living. I felt so alone, as if I was the only person on the planet.

'I thought of some of me friends who were less lucky, like Paddy Smith from South Tipp whose body had just been found in a wood. A dacent man with whom I'd shared many a trench joke and fright. It was hard to believe he was gone. But, as I remembered Paddy, I came to realise how lucky I was. Black and blue I might be, but I was still in one piece. I'd probably be left alone now, thanks to the PP. And I still had me Angelus picture.

'I got up and made a cup of tay. I had to sit down carefully outside the door, they'd kicked me where I'd been wounded. As I swallowed the first draught, I thought 'twas the nicest cup I'd ever drank. Me head was spinning with the shock, me bottom ached, but I knew 'twould be all right in a few days. I looked up at the big sky and the stars all in their usual places. They'd seen everything from the dawn of time, they'd outlive all the lunacy. I was comforted, the fear left me shoulders. I finished me pipeful, went inside and slept soundly. I felt everything would be all right. From now on, I could start living again.'

'I'm sorry, Dan. I did not know that people could be so cruel. I never heard about these things from my parents or anyone else. I was only told of all the crimes the English had committed. You are a great man, you have survived two wars.'

'The Romans said nothing bad about the Romans – it's the winners who write the histories,' the Gunner stood up. 'I'm glad to get all that off me chest. Thirty year of silence wore me down, with none I could trust enough to tell me story to. Cut off from everyone, always on guard, I felt I was still fighting. Now, having shared it, I feel me war may finally be ending. But, with all the talking, the bloody drink's gone cold, I'll brew some more.'

Salvo peered expectantly from the flagstone. 'Some apple for you too, me friend,' Dan emerged. 'I recovered from a crock leg and so will you, we'll unearth some more nourishing worms this evening in me garden.

'Like Salvo, an army marches on its stomach – do you know who said that? Napoleon. He conquered half of Europe until our man Wellington put a stop to his gallop at Waterloo. And now who remembers either of them? 'Twill be the same one day with me own war and all me poor comrades who were slaughtered. But the sun's shining, we'll enjoy it and our tay. Did you ever hear the saying that life's like a good cuppa, it's all in how you make it? We must put the bad things behind us and get on with our lives.'

'But, were you not sad at losing your medals, after all you had been through to win them?'

'Sad? The divil a bit,' the Gunner flung the dregs of his tea far out on the grass in front of them.

'I wasn't as cracked as they thought I was. When I was coming home through London from the war, I bought a set of joke medals at Petticoat Lane market. I was going to give them to Paddy Dwyer, so he could march up and down and pretend he'd been in the trenches too. But I came back to a country where there was no more fun. I thought to meself, they can kill me, but they won't get me decorations. I hid them one night, together with some sovereigns I'd bought with me paying-off allowance. The medals me visitors got were the dummy ones.'

'But if they came back and found the real ones, you would have been in big trouble?'

'I'm afraid they couldn't,' Dan shook his head. 'I wrapped them up well in waterproof cloth and buried them above in the rath. So, whenever I hear people arguing about whether or not there's gold there, I laugh to meself. I know there is.'

'Now that there are no more gunmen, all you have to do is get a spade and dig them up. I would love to see them.'

'Not as much as I would. I promised them I'd be back and I will. Trouble is, I can't pinpoint the hiding spot. I dug holes near the left-side trees, so many steps forwards, so many to the left. But I was always in too much of a hurry, still nervous that someone might see me.'

The Gunner covered his face with his hand. 'Fighting destroys people and war and fear does terrible things to your brain.'

He jumped up and starting pacing around. 'Ireland's worst day was when the hooligans took over. Behind a gun, nobodies became God Almighty overnight. Common sense and humanity went out the door, anti-violence was considered anti-Irish. Their killing and new power were like drugs, they couldn't stop. When the British left, they turned on each other. Some families here still don't speak to each other because of the Civil War. If I hadn't been frightened be madcaps like them, I might have dug up me medals long ago.'

'It is all right, Dan. The fighting is over now. I am sure there is a way they can be found, if we put our minds to it.'

'Half the people here think I'm soft in the head,' the Gunner paused for breath. 'So would they, if they were bombarded be bombs for years. They're so short on the imagination, 'tis nearly comical.'

His brow relaxed, he sat down slowly. 'Others often ask why I'm so merry at times. When I wake up in the morning and it's quiet and I see the fields warming in the sun, I know how lucky I am. Every day without the whine of a bullet is a day to celebrate. Only yesterday, Molly Barney was giving out about the weather. "More rain again tomorrow, we'll all soon have webbed feet, Dan."

'I told her I often felt the same until poor Ron from Manchester was killed beside me be a sniper. The heavens opened next day. I was feeling sorry for meself, until it hit me that Ron would never feel the rain again.

' "It can pour in bucketfuls as far as I'm concerned, Molly," I said. "As long as I can feel it, I know I'm in one piece. Aren't we lucky to be able to feel the rain?"

'She's still looking at me.'

Dan took off his cap and scratched his head. 'Our time's limited, like a soldier's rum ration. We should enjoy it before it's snatched away again. I've come to the conclusion that most people are only sleep-walking. Wasting their energy worrying about money or what might happen the year after next. They don't appreciate the wealth around them, like those slopes our midlands neighbours would die for. I tell them how lucky they are to be able to smell the lilac, that they should knock a tune out of the day that's in it. When I say this, people only laugh at me like Molly. I sometimes wonder if they're the cuckoo ones.'

'You are right, Dan. You are a wise man and a clever one to fool your visitors. Do you still miss the medals?'

'I think about them every day, it's the hope of recovering them that keeps me going. It took some time for things to cool down. I didn't feel 'twas safe to start looking properly until around ten year ago. I dug every summer since then, you can still see the patches. I'd no luck, but I won't rest 'til I find them.'

Having read so much about buried treasure, there was nothing the boy would like more than to be involved in a real-life hunt. 'Well, Dan, maybe it is time to start a thorough search. It is great that you saved them and that they are still up there. I will study my books and see if I can get some advice about digging. You should have a plan to give you the best chance of finding them.'

'Plans? I had me bellyful of them in the war, thank you. Forget the paperwork, it's elbow grease that gets things done. And don't forget what I said about not telling anyone.'

As he walked home, the boy pictured the Gunner burying his hard-earned decorations. All he had to show for the conflict, apart from shell-shock and his limp. Stumbling up the moonlit slope, looking over his shoulder to see if anyone was following. Being threatened and humiliated by men he himself knew in their village. These now seemed far from the freedom-loving patriots he had been taught to believe in. And then being unable to talk about it for so long. Reflecting on all his friend had endured strengthened his determination to support him. He hoped Dan would ask for his assistance. But, if he did, how would he get around his mother, who not only restricted his playing but would certainly not allow him to search for British war medals?

4.

Starting the Search

*'With the ould health up and down, it
could be now or never.'*

'The Gunner said you were good company,
you can go down after lunch,' his mother
told him on Sunday morning. 'But for two hours
only.'

As he opened the front door, he could hear
the cheers from Casey's garage across the street.
On the days of the big hurling and football finals,
Dick propped up the front window so that vil-
lagers could listen to the wireless commentaries.
He would like to hear the match, but he wanted
to help the Gunner more. 'He's forty yards out.
He's sidestepped the half-backs. It's an impossible

48

angle. But it's over the bar, Christy Ring, another point for Cork. The cup is almost in their hands.'

Would similar success attend the equally challenging task of unearthing the Gunner's trophies? Climbing to Dan's house, he wondered how he liked living near a place which was said to have been once the home of the fairies.

'I've yet to meet the little people,' the Gunner looked up the hill.

'But for me the rath has always been a magical place. Particularly on the days after me uninvited guests, when I jumped at every sound and wondered if me troubles would ever be over. It saved me life. The trees sheltered me from everything, the bright furze cheered me up. How lucky I was to be able to hear the birds, unlike mates who'd been deafened be the big guns. And though I might limp, I could walk, unlike many who'd lost their legs. I realised then that I should be counting me blessings.

'In time, the people changed too. After four or five year, villagers didn't cross the road anymore to avoid me. I got jobs here and there. Neighbours gave me turf for the fire in return for helping in the bog. The only ones I avoided were those who'd raided me house. They made up for it by telling everyone I was cracked, they'd no idea I'd fooled them. I spent Sundays at the playing field and was soon carrying the jerseys for the hurling team. We'd great fun, cycling off to Nenagh, Borrisoleigh and Moneygall, singing the latest ballads:

Hay and oats for the Moneygall goats,
Eggs and rashers for the Toomevara dashers.

'It might have been better for me search if I'd written down the directions. But, if I'd done that, those men might have found them. I dug everywhere I was sure the box was, but it wasn't. The years play tricks on your memory. Though times had changed, I still worried that people might discover what I was up to.

' "Are you after buried treasure?" Dick Casey was walking there one day.

' "I'm thinking of a treasure of turnips, the rath would be a great place to grow them," I told him.

'Come around here and I'll show you something,' Dan led him to the back of his house.

'What do you think of me new spade? Strong and sharp and the right size for getting under any roots. Bill O'Meara will drop in a crowbar at the weekend. Now that summer's back, I'm starting me final search. This time, I'll keep going 'til I find them. I could do with some help. If you'd like to join me during the holidays, you'd be very welcome.'

'Dan, I thought you'd never ask. Count me in. My mother always says two heads are better than one. I am free from now until August, apart from some study for the new school.'

'You'll get a bounty for any help, maybe even something from me hoard.'

'My reward will be seeing you get everything back after all you did in the war, Dan. No time like the present. Will we go and have a look in the rath – exactly the same way you went that night?'

'It was this time of the year with the blossoms on the hawthorns that I came up here with me medals,' the Gunner led the way.

'But, like the oak, the rath seems fuller now than it did then. Nature never stands still, a lot happens in a few year. There's more furze and more trees. The badger holes were not here before. If those fellas got their teeth into me biscuit tin, they'd be promenading with me medals every night.'

The Gunner pushed his way inside and walked forward ten paces. "Twas around here, as far as I can remember. The heap of stones was just about there in front of us, and the young hawthorn ten paces to the left, about twenty foot. I dug the hole two foot deep in the middle of the two spots.'

The rath was about seventy feet in diameter. There were several mature hawthorns and, on the left edge, the oak from which he had surveyed their village. The floor was uneven. Like snakes scurrying underground, roots swirled in all directions. Bleached patches marked the sites of the Gunner's earlier excavations. A heap of large reddish stones bordered the eastern slope facing Carroll's hurling field. Could he remember seeing the village or any other landmark while he was digging?

'The trees which sheltered me hid everything else. All I remember is the shadow the midnight moon made on those rocks to me right. I got such a start when it stood up the same time as me. When I'd buried me treasures, I scurried down the hill as quickly as I could. So exposed, I felt as if I was in no-man's land again. Waiting for the rattle of a machine gun that would end everything.'

'Dan, I will come back tomorrow and we will have a better look around. My mother thinks I might be bothering you, maybe you could call to the house and pick me up?'

Walking home, he pondered how to organise their search. Despite what the Gunner thought, they should not dig at random, they would have to have a strategy. But how could he persuade Dan that this was the best approach? He would con-

52

sult his adventure books for advice. And, when his mother let him up again, he would complete his sketch of the rath.

The Gunner called after lunch the following day. 'He can go and play for a couple of hours. Better than idling here and pestering me with questions about everything,' his mother greeted him. 'But, no climbing and make sure he is back early to do some studying. The harder he works, the sooner he can see you again.'

'We'd all be still above in the same trees, mam, if we hadn't asked questions,' Dan chuckled.

The boy could not wait to get up to the rath. He thought the Gunner felt the same, he seemed livelier than he had been for a long time. 'You're like Sherlock Holmes looking for clues, all you need is the deerstalker,' Dan watched, as he pulled the jotter from under his jersey and started pacing up and down.

He noted where each tree and indentation was. And Dan's entrance route that distant night. But, where had the rocks been, there was not even one anywhere near the hawthorn trees? The Gunner pointed eastwards. 'Most were bigger than me fist but the children who played here years ago carried them over there to build a wall. That pile's what's left of their wall now. If they'd left the bloody things where they were before, we'd have been in business.'

'Do not worry, Dan, your treasure is still here and we will find it. The stones would have been a great landmark but we will get around that. I will go home and draw a proper map to help find the best place to dig.'

'Another sketch, you are reading far too much of those pirate stories,' his mother saw him drawing that evening. 'But I suppose playing on the hill is safer than falling around in the river.'

He drew a straight line from the Gunner's house up to the rath, before sketching in the outer rim of furze. Marking north and south, he mapped the nearest trees and bushes. He circled the left-hand ground between the first hawthorns and the point where the Gunner thought he had entered. That would be their search area. But where to start? As the Gunner was so sure about the young hawthorn, they should first dig near one of the mature ones. He would decide which one when he returned next day. His plan completed, he took out his geography books.

'You studied last night, off you go to the hill again if you want,' his mother surprised him after breakfast on Tuesday.

She would not have been so amenable had she been aware of his medals mission. He felt guilty for concealing the search from his mother. But if he told her, she would put her foot down and they might never find Dan's decorations. Surely that was the most important consideration?

'We're lucky with the weather,' the Gunner was standing by his door.

'As your father would have told you from making potato drills, dry weather's tops for digging. We've the best tools, we'll search until we find me hoard. Let's go.'

He was as excited as the Gunner, as they walked up the slope. He was going on a secret mission that only Dan and he knew about. Sun reflections flashed from the Gunner's crowbar, while he carried the spade over his right shoulder. Once inside the furze, the Gunner took ten steps forward. 'It's around here to the left that I buried them. You're the only one to help me, you excavate first,' he leaned on the bar in the shadow of the oak.

The spade only penetrated a few inches, the clay was more compacted than in his father's garden.

'I thought as much,' the Gunner steadied his crowbar. 'I'll open it up for you first. Then you'll be like President O'Kelly, planting a memorial tree in a hole that's already been made.'

The loosened earth was easier to dig, within an hour they were down almost two feet. But all they had to show for their efforts was a mound of dark clay. 'Well, they're not here,' the Gunner wiped his brow. 'I wonder if anyone might have come up and taken them?'

'Dan, this is only our first attempt. No one apart from yourself knew they were buried here. We have nothing to worry about, they are still here somewhere.'

They extended the hole for another hour, but found nothing. Tommy Barney's Angelus bell rang across the fields, as they started to fill in the trench. 'Nearly lunchtime, Dan, I will go home now for an hour and keep my mother happy,' he patted the fresh clay.

They might not have unearthed the medals but, as they looked back, they saw yellow beaks flashing, as two blackbirds feasted on the worms they had turned up. 'Treasure for our patient friends, maybe that's a good sign,' Dan led him out.

'You have finished your lunch, miracles,' his mother cleared the plates. 'Off you go again but be back at half past five. The Gunner is great to be keeping an eye on you, tell him I will have some fresh soda cake for him in a couple of days.'

Keeping secrets was hard work. 'Dan always looks forward to your baking,' he tightened his boot laces and set off as casually as he could.

When he reached the rath, the Gunner was already breaking up the ground. 'We'll keep going to the left, then the other way and we're bound to strike gold,' Dan handed him the spade.

As the Gunner rested the crowbar, he removed the earth. Soon, their trench was three feet long.

'I hope no one comes up, they'll think we're planning a murder,' Dan looked around. 'Like Dick Casey, I'll give them the turnips yarn.'

The work was tiring in the sun. 'Break time,' the Gunner led the way down to his house.

The boy felt like an adult after a hard day's work, as he sat down. 'Your seat is like a throne, Dan. I hope I can have a house with a view like this when I grow up.'

'I'm sure you'll find your home, you've the dream, that's the start, that's more important than money. If you don't have dreams, who else will have them for you? Life's full of possibilities. Doc Murphy said to me the other day; "When you're dying, you'll kick yourself not for what you did, but for what you didn't do."

'So, don't be afraid, don't wait for things to happen, try everything. And, if you make mistakes, that's progress. There's no bad experience from which you don't learn. The world would have stood still, if people had not dreamt.'

'You never gave up hope of recovering your medals, Dan, and now we are on the way to realising that.'

'Dreams have to be lubricated too – with good old-fashioned elbow grease,' the Gunner waved a mottled arm. 'Stick that in your jotter as well.'

He felt that Dan still doubted his maps and plans. They started up the slope. 'We'll try the other way now,' the Gunner applied his crowbar.

They dug for another hour. But, the lower they went, the denser the soil became. Even manoeuvring the bar was difficult. 'There's something here, something stopping the crowbar,' the Gunner rocked from side to side. 'It's moving, I've shifted it. Get the spade down there quickly.'

Growing as excited as the Gunner, he dug out the clay. At the third effort, he felt the object and managed to get the spade under it. It was the skull of a long-dead animal.

'A sheep be the looks of it. For a minute, I thought we were onto something,' the Gunner leaned on his crowbar.

Digging for buried treasure was harder than they had suggested in the books. 'I will see you in the morning, Dan,' he brushed the clay off his boots.

After supper, he consulted *Treasure Island* for more ideas on searching. It was his favourite adventure book, bought for him one Christmas by the Gunner himself. Only the better-off children got holiday presents. But St. Stephen's Day gave the rest the opportunity to collect scarce pennies, as they went around from house to house singing 'The wren, the wren. The king of all birds. On St Stephen's Day he was caught in the furze.'

The king of all the wrenboys was the Gunner. Each year, he dressed up in a black mask and red coat and leaped through the street waving a long wooden staff. Everyone came to their doors to see him. By the time he reached the barracks, the village children were dancing behind him. 'The Pied Piper', his mother called him.

He took more money than the other wrenboys put together, before treating them all to lemonade in Harty's. But they ran away from him afterwards, as he staggered from pub to pub singing 'Pack up your troubles in your old kit-bag, and smile, smile, smile.'

'You can't bate Christmas, like armistice day in Wipers,' he leaned against their door after the last Wren Day. 'Mam, I've made a few bob. Can I take this son of yours across to Tierney's and we'll see if we can get him a nice book?'

'I've never seen anyone with a greater appreciation of money – or less regard for it,' his mother shook her head.

'It's made round to go around,' the Gunner dragged him into the shop opposite their house. 'Now, pick whatever book you like. The bigger the better. How about that red one with the pirates on it?'

It would be nice to repay Dan for his kindness.

Tomorrow, he hoped, they would make good progress.

5.

A Great Day for Excavating

*For the first time, he thought his
mother was wrong*

The Gunner was waiting on the road for him when he arrived on Wednesday morning.

'We won't waste any time. Another good day for working, but not so fine tomorrow,' he pointed to the clouds massing behind Keeper. 'But by then, maybe, we'll have found our treasure. We'll try to the right today, let's go.'

The ground was as demanding as before. Supporting himself on his good leg, the Gunner rotated the crowbar, while he removed the clay. 'Bloody flies,' Dan waved his hand and pushed his cap down to protect against the sun.

They had now established a routine. Every time he rested his spade, the Gunner lowered his crowbar and loosened the earth. They dug more quickly than the previous day, soon their new trench was a yard long. But they unearthed nothing more substantial than decayed roots and animal bones. The Angelus bell rang, he headed down the hill to home. He could smell the boiled bacon and cabbage, as he entered the door.

'The mountain air again,' his mother looked at his empty plate. 'You can go back now but tomorrow stay at home and study.'

He did not mind. If they found nothing today and if it rained, as Dan had forecast, it would give him time to plan a better search.

'We'll go forwards this time,' the Gunner loosened the front edge of the trench. 'We'll do as much as we can, before the heavens open.'

He felt something solid as he removed the loose clay. Could this be the Gunner's treasure? But he was unable to shift it. 'Have a look at this Dan.'

The Gunner levered, then knelt for a closer inspection. 'Nothing of mine, I'm afraid. It's the end of a root from the big tree there. If one of those could stretch that distance, what could it do to me poor biscuit tin? But, no problem, we'll dig around it.'

After another ten minutes, Dan rested his crowbar. 'Wouldn't we save a lot of time and shoulder ache if we'd a digging machine? With the technology we've already here in the village, it should be possible to invent one. Isn't it great the way Matt Boland harnesses the river to drive his turbine and saw timber and grind corn. He makes animal food for the farmers, even the oats I have every morning. As well as charging batteries for the lampers who hunt the rabbits. Maybe, we should ask him to make us an excavator?'

'If we do that, Dan, everyone will know our business.'

'You're a sharp one, we'll stick with the human machines,' the Gunner gripped his crowbar.

They dug for another hour. The clay piled up in front of them but their only reward was an old whiskey flask. The sky darkened. 'We'll have to call it a day,' Dan stopped. 'Treasure hunting's hard work. You go home and have a good rest. I'll drop into FrenchShea's tonight for a medicinal pint. We'll do nothing for a few days until the ground dries out.'

A familiar bird fluttered ahead of them, as they descended. 'Miracles, I think he's on the mend,' Dan slowed.

'You are Toome's Saint Francis,' the boy propped his spade against the back wall of the house.

'Free music from dawn 'til dusk, I'm only re-paying a debt when I look after this fella.

'He's not me only mate. There's Mr Spotty, the thrush who studies me digging the garden every evening. A flock of sparrows have a dustbath each morning outside the door. Every summer, I watch the swallows dive along the street and over the river, before darting up to their nests under Looby's eaves. Do you know, they don't stop to eat like the others, they catch their insects on the wing? And, when the days draw in, they're off to Africa and don't return 'til it's nice and warm here again. How they find their way back every year to the same nests, I'll never understand – and man thinks he's the clever one.

'And did you ever hear anything to match their music? Though I'd love to have a gramo-phone, who needs a machine when you've got the birds? And the smaller they are, like the wren and the blue tit, the sweeter their song. The only ones I hate are the crows. With their joyless squawking and the way they congregate like an army every evening, before flying off to the Shelley's Cross trees. I saw too many of them during the war, tearing at dead horses and even the bodies of poor unburied soldiers. The sight and sound of them brings bad memories...'

The Gunner tapped himself on the head. 'Salvo, your saucer. I must be getting old, I'm forgetting too many bloody things.'

Two days' work without any result. Treasure hunting demanded perseverance, as well as application. Walking home, he recalled the Gunner remarking how far the furze had spread over the years. 'It's out at least two foot more in all directions.'

His own memory was as bad as Dan's, why had he not recalled this earlier? Little wonder they had found nothing, they had been searching in the wrong place. They should have taken off two feet before measuring into the rath. He would revisit his calculations.

'Cats and dogs, no playing today,' his mother confirmed the Gunner's forecast the following morning from their porch. 'The best time for revision.'

He went out to have a look. The road ran with muddy rivulets. Rain lashed the windows and washed away an old swallow's nest under Looby's roof. It poured down from the eaves of the hall and from Jim O'Rourke's green cape and cap, as he delivered the post. Armstrongs' thatched roof would be soaked, he hoped it would not fall in.

No longer a gentle stream, he could hear the river as it rushed out from under the bridge. It would easily sweep away the last dam he had made. It seemed such a long time since he had played there.

Remembering the Gunner's advice to turn disadvantage to advantage, he had his history books out when his mother came into the dining room. 'Do you think the Tuatha de Dannan really lived on the Gunner's hill?' he enquired.

'There is no written evidence. But, legends can sometimes be true, Homer's poems led archaeologists to long-lost Greek sites. One day, they may investigate the rath and then we will know for sure. Meantime, learn what you can now and you will be ahead of the other scholars when you start secondary school. I heard the Gunner is digging drills up there to grow turnips. Maybe, he might prove those stories true and turn up a bit of treasure yet?' she gave him a sideways look.

If she only knew, he thought. Did she suspect something? He felt ashamed for not letting her into the secret, but he had promised the Gunner. Soon enough, hopefully, she would be the first in the village to hear the big news.

The water flashed rainbow colours as he leaned over the sun-warmed river wall on Saturday morning. How the weather could change so much in such a short time. The village seemed so fresh and crisp, as if it had been washed clean. But he was in no hurry to return to the rath, the Gunner had said it would take at least three days for the ground to dry. 'Time for a late Spring Clean,' his mother called him into the sitting room.

She removed the throws from the sofa and chairs. He helped her carry out the blankets for airing. 'The Gunner does not have any nice coverings,' he fastened the clothes pegs.

'Do not worry,' she secured the last one. 'We will buy some more in Nenagh next week. Then, he can have these, as well as a couple of new mugs to celebrate the summer.'

His mother was kind to poorer villagers. Though she disapproved of drinking, every year she gave Dan and Paddy Dwyer a couple of bottles of stout each, as well as a corner of the Christmas cake. How was it, then, that she sympathised with the men who had frightened the Gunner and might have even killed him?

'As Bill O'Meara said, 'tis all an accident of birth, people usually follow what they're brought up in,' Dan had told him one day. 'Even intelligent folk can be led astray be clever talk. People lose all sense when they get into nationalism or any other ism. When I'm in power, all isms will be banned. If they only stood back and asked questions, they'd soon realise we're all the same under the skin. They'd see that if we worked together, instead of fighting each other, the world would be a better place. I'm convinced people have the same amount of good in them as bad. They're just waiting for the nod to use one or the other.

'During the last bad summer, everyone here – rich, poor, young, old, Catholic and Protestant – all came together to save the harvest. Tilly lamps swayed on the horse-drawn reapers and binders into the late hours. Teams of villagers dodged the threshing machine belts, as they cut the sheaves and filled the bags with wheat. People had never had such fun, nor worked as hard. It brought out the best in everyone. I wish it could always be like that. Then we'd have no wars – and I'd be in me full health as well.'

The harvesting had also provided a new adventure for the boy. He was allowed to join the adults and other schoolchildren in nearby fields. As well as staying up late and learning rude words he had never heard at home, he was rewarded with sandwiches and lemonade at Donovan's and other farms. The government also paid villagers to catch rabbits. 'It's like the Aurora

Borealis,' Paddy Dwyer said as lamp beams swept the countryside.

After they had finished the cleaning, his mother opened the glass bookcase which his father had made. She read many books since she had to resign from school-teaching when she married. 'Worrying about the Sergeant out all night guarding a disputed farm is bad enough. But giving up my own work was just as hard, I do not think I will ever get over it,' he had once overheard her telling Tom MacDonald.

'Study this and learn something about your country's history,' she removed her apron and handed him *Tipperary's Fighting Story*.

But, as he read, he began to wonder if his mother's heroes were really so gallant after all. One boasted of shooting unarmed policemen. 'These are the people who killed those two men on our square. Surely that was as cruel as anything the British had done?' he startled her.

She lowered her Ethel Mannin novel. 'I will let you off this time, but never again say anything like that about the brave men who freed our country.'

He knew now he would be in real trouble if she discovered his medals quest. 'But how can it be brave to shoot defenceless men in the back?' he persisted. 'Do not the Commandments say: "Thou shall not kill"?'

She waved the book at him. 'Now, that is enough, do not upset me any more. The past is the past, we must get on with our lives. There are many things that you are too young to understand.'

For the first time, he thought his mother was wrong. For the first time, he began to question some of the things he had been brought up to believe. He wondered if the Gunner had been right. His parents and he could so easily have been born in a different country. 'If your mother grew up across the water, she'd be Protestant and flapping a red, white and blue flag, not green and orange.'

His mother waving a Union Jack, he was shocked. But after thinking about it, he had to agree with Dan. So why did people mistrust each other so much, when we were really all the same? And why was England blamed for everything, when it provided work for so many villagers? He had seen parents regularly crying at the bus stop, as sons and daughters departed for Liverpool or London, clutching their brown paper parcels of belongings. Keeping half the village going, how could England be the awful place his mother insisted it was? Even she laughed, when the Gunner remarked one evening 'Now, mam, we can't be holding King George responsible for the bad weather.'

Dan had also discussed religion with his mother. 'I'm not so sure about the church these days. All the talk about love and charity and the rest of it. But Protestant Harry Brown had to convert to marry Kathleen Ryan a fortnight ago, and promise all their children would be brought up as Catholics. And now none of his family will speak to him. Two religions in the parish, both supposed to be Christian, but each looking down on the other. That's not very Christian?'

'Those are the rules, Dan, and they must be obeyed.'

'Rules? I heard a lot of them in nineteen and fourteen, mam.'

Doctor Murphy called that night. 'Dan has slowed lately,' he sank into the front-room settee.

'No human mind or body could withstand that constant shelling and thunder of heavy guns. Shell-shock is one of the war's worst legacies, the shock waves caused concussion and brain damage. It resulted in panic attacks, insomnia, hypersensitivity to noise. You knew where you were with a missing limb, with shell-shock the damage was not so obvious. The lads who came back looked just like the young men who had left years earlier. But they were not. They were changed terribly, they had witnessed and endured unimaginable horrors.'

'Many of them must have been mentally damaged,' his father put down his cup.

'You are right, Sergeant. Who would be normal, after being through all that? Since independence, the Great War is not taught in our schools. Consequently, few now either know or care about the soldiers' sacrifices, or the killing of so many after they returned. The forgotten generation. Unlike those hospitalised in England, Dan has never had specialist treatment. He is still subject to moods and depressions, he deserves great credit for battling it all alone. It would help if you can ever listen to his experiences. I told him my door is always open to him – he has taken me at my word on many a late night. Despite everything, he has never lost his sense of humour. The other night, he quoted something Bill O'Meara had told him; "War does not determine who is right – only who is left." '

'Good to see you are not neglecting your arithmetic,' his mother leaned over his shoulder on Sunday evening. 'Two days in a row, well done. As you have been so studious, you can go back and see the Gunner tomorrow, but make sure you take a pair of old boots this time.'

Had she been more observant, she would have noticed the sketch of the rath, marked with a new X to show where excavations should resume. He was confident he was at last on the right track.

6.

Remembering the War

'There are times when I can't fight any longer.'

'We made a mistake with our measurements,' he took his spade from the Gunner on Monday morning. 'We did not allow for the spread of the furze.'

Dan removed his cap. 'How the hell could I have forgotten that?'

They restarted two feet back from their first trench. It seemed a little too far from the trees the Gunner had originally described. 'If only those stones were still in their original place,' Dan shook his head

Nearer to the furze, the digging seemed easier. Magpies strutted and squawked on the em-

74

bankment as they worked. They excavated for over an hour and then extended the hole to the left. He was getting stronger, he was pleased to find the work much easier than on the first days. They found no treasure but they were rewarded with a rusted tobacco tin and part of an old clay pipe. 'So, I wasn't the first to come up here and have a smoke', the Gunner scraped the earth off the broken stem.

Later that afternoon, the Gunner peered into the expanding trench. 'Now, there's a rare relic', he reached down.

It was the rest of the clay pipe. Its scorched bowl featured a man's head. 'Charles Stewart Parnell, one of the best', the Gunner cleaned it against a trouser-leg.

'My mother has a medal of him at home. She would be delighted to see this, she often talks about Parnell.'

'Well, she's right there. A Protestant, he took on the might of Westminster and secured more for us than all the sharpshooters put together. Like Dr Noel Browne, who's just rid us of the scourge of TB. Say nothing about this for the time being, but maybe, we could give her the pipe after we find our own treasure? Come down for a cuppa and I'll tell you a bit about history nearer home.'

'We haven't forgotten you this time, Salvo,' he brought out a handful of crumbs and a mug of water for the bird's saucer. 'Keep eating, you're getting there. Join me in the garden later for your afters.'

Was there anything to beat tea outdoors after hard work? Dan made himself comfortable on the grass and lit his pipe. 'Do you know, there's an ocean of history down there and in the village behind us?' he pointed the pipe stem.

'A legacy of accomplishment that many places would envy. Though some don't appreciate it, isn't Toome the real McCoy of villages? Sitting under those hills, with the river flowing through the centre. And the bridge, mill pond and a pair of churches to keep us on the straight and narrow. Seven centuries old, that abbey on the square is said to have replaced a wooden church built after St Patrick died. The Augustinian ruins beside the chapel have been there for as long. Four hundred years ago at Aghnameadle, the MacEgans had a college in which scholars from the four corners studied everything from history to law and poetry.'

Dan gestured to their left. 'Before he went off to Iona with Columba, St Odhran had an even older monastery and school in Latteragh, where the Toome river rises. Wouldn't it be great if people here thought more about this history than all that ould bang-bang stuff? And, if it was better known, it could do wonders for the place. Imagine tourists pouring in – wouldn't it restore our pride and give the whole place a lift? And, the more visitors, the more spondulix for everyone. I might even make a few bob meself, showing Yanks where the Tuatha De Danann lived. Naturally, I'd remind them that me own name's the same as the De Danann goddess, Danu.

'No one knows more about local history than Paddy and Bill O'Meara, friends of Katherine Guilfoyle who became a poet in America. From a great sporting family, they could tell you everything about the Toomevara Greyhounds, one of the best hurling teams ever seen in Ireland. Bill showed me where the Bianconi coaches stopped here in the 1800s, Ireland's first coach service. Paddy told me how Barry O'Meara of Lissniskey House, a couple of miles away, became Napoleon's doctor. Paddy and fellow-teacher Tom MacDonald published *The Spirit of Tipperary*, the poetry and learning of the county over the centuries. Including our own man from Grenanstown, Richard Dalton Williams. Let me show you something Bill gave me.'

The Gunner limped inside and returned with his only book, the mildewed *Poems of Richard Dalton Williams*. Published in Dublin in 1894, a faded embossed gold harp decorated its frayed green cover. 'As you know, I can only make out the big letters. But Bill read me "The Dying Girl" one evening, 'twould make you proud to be a Tipp man. I learned it be heart, I'll recite it for you:

> From a Munster vale they brought her.
> From the pure and balmy air;
> An Ormond peasant's daughter,
> With blue eyes and Golden hair.
> They brought her to the city,
> And she faded slowly there –
> Consumption has no pity
> For blue eyes and golden hair.

'Do you know the poem was based on a local girl Williams had treated in Dublin? Bill tramped with me over to Kilkeary one day and showed me her grave on the site of an ancient nunnery. Mary Feely, only twenty when she passed away in 1845. Wasn't it sad that, doctor and all, poor Williams died of tuberculosis at the age of thirty-nine? In Louisiana, a long way from Toomevara.'

The Gunner put the book down and pointed to their right. 'And there's more history just across there. Bill told me how those archaeologists have found long-forgotten sites be going up in aeroplanes. From high above, they can see traces you can't notice when you're walking down below. But, you can also read the past while on the ground. When the sun sets at an angle over that field beside the priest's house, you can see ridges and humps. All that's left of the shacks from which poor locals were evicted a hundred year ago. Before the famine there were nine hundred living in Toome, by 1851 there were only four hundred left. Newcomers took land that wasn't theirs, which might explain the whispering and suspicion you don't find in other villages.'

A poetry and history lesson on the side of a hill, the boy felt he had learned more from the Gunner than he had from his schoolbooks.

'Do not let appearances deceive you, Dan is one of the wisest men around,' Doctor Murphy insisted in their house one night. 'His experiences have made him an outsider, he can observe things more clearly than the rest of us. His lack of education has made him more curious than most, he loves knowledge for its own sake. He is a graduate of the best college of all, the university of life.'

But history lessons were not going to find the medals. They climbed back to the rath. The sun on their shoulders, they worked their way to the right. Dan crowbarred, he dug. With every spadeful, he felt they must be getting closer to their goal. Twice, they struck something solid. Each time, he thought it might be their treasure. But, their discoveries turned out to be more large stones. He sensed that the Gunner was disappointed, he worried again about his recollections. Those rocks would have been their best guide. 'Your medals are here somewhere, Dan, we will find them,' he started to fill in the trench. 'I will go home and restudy my map.'

'You're a great help to me, but I'm not so sure anymore about plans and paperwork,' the Gunner scratched his head. 'We've tried all that without any result. I think I'll go back to me own way, to what me memory and me gut tell me.'

'Dan, my father says that, unlike the Pope, memories are not infallible. To recollect something accurately after many years is very hard. Even after ten minutes, accident witnesses change their stories. And don't forget how much the rath has also altered in that time.'

'You can say that again. As well as the furze, the little trees I saw are all now so big and those stones were moved. But me instincts have never let me down yet. They helped me survive the war and everything else. I'll go back to the old-fashioned digging in what I think is the right place.'

His first disagreement with the Gunner, he was unsure how to handle it. 'Dan, you did that for ten years without success. And, as you say, the rath is not what it was before. If I can include those changes in my map, it will give us a clearer picture based on facts. That might be more reliable than memory.'

'I'm beginning to feel sorry I ever bought you that treasure book, but you're a trier, God bless you,' the Gunner dried his sweating palms on his trousers. 'You're taking after the Sergeant, a divil for the facts. We'll think about it for a few days. And I might have some refreshments tonight, treasure hunting's thirsty work. Does herself have any idea what we're up to yet?'

❧ ❧ ❧

'No hill for a couple of days,' the boy's mother ladled out his porridge next morning. 'Dan went on the tear last night, he will be in no mood for visitors. I do not know why he spends it all in Harty's and FrenchShea's, making them rich, while he gets poorer and slower.'

He had noticed that the Gunner was not rushing around as he used to. Or taking such long steps. But, how slow he had been himself. Not to realise that this would also have affected their measurements. He sharpened his pencil and set to work on his jotter. The Gunner said that when burying the medals, he had taken ten steps into the rath, about twenty feet. Then around ten more steps, he had thought, to the left. But his new shorter footsteps meant that they had only measured out about three-quarters of that distance. A difference of up to five feet, a big discrepancy. Better late than never, he thought, and penned a new X on his map.

'Will himself be down in the morning?' Dan knocked on Thursday evening.

'I suppose he can, he has been helping me lately, come in and have a cup of tea,' his mother opened the door.

'A great lad, he'd have been a sound ally on the Front. But I hope he never has to go through all that.'

'It must be difficult to forget the war?' his mother poured.

'It's hard work to put it all out of the mind, that's why I take a jar sometimes,' Dan paused his cup.

> 'Seven glasses used to be
> Called for six good mates and me –
> Now, we only call for three...

'But I had to learn to forget, otherwise I'd have gone under like so many others. One of me worst experiences was returning to France after a fortnight's leave. Imagine exchanging the quiet of Toome for the bedlam of the Front. No pillow to rest me head on over there. No roof to keep out the elements, the same clothes for months. Always on the move, like a can being kicked hither and thither be Generals we never saw. With people being killed left, right and centre. And the quiet days as anxious, with time to think that the luck which had so far saved me must soon run out.'

'What was your most dangerous experience, Dan?'

'I was trapped in no man's land after we'd gone over the top one morning. I'll never forget it. 'Twas like being in the middle of a million swarms of bees. Bullets whizzing all around, stones blasting us from shell bursts. The rat-tat-tat of the machine guns was terrible. Within a minute, they'd cut the entire platoon to bits. Fellas were screaming on all sides of me. I was shot in the hip, bowled over as if I'd been hit be a dozen hurley sticks. That's what left me with the limp.

'I stopped the blood with an old handkerchief, and lay doggo between the bodies of lads I'd joked with minutes earlier. The gaz was everyone's worst nightmare, I was lucky, I caught only a bit of it. As night came on, I could see the Plough and all the stars above. I wondered if anyone in Toome was looking up at them at the same time. I was a Long Long Way from Tipperary all right, I didn't think I would see Keeper again.

'I'd to work hard to stop meself crying with the pain. If the Huns had heard me, they'd have come and finished me off. I don't mind telling you that at one stage I was tempted just to give in. No more fear, no more bombs, rest at last. But 'twas too easy a way out, I didn't want to give me life away without a fight. I thought about me own peaceful village, I hung on. Ten hours after being hit, I finally stood up and crawled back towards our own lines. Hoping at every step I wouldn't be mistaken for the enemy and be shot be one of me own. You could say that was the worst day of me life. But 'twas also one of the best. I'd discovered what a precious gift life was.'

'You must have been glad to finally get home safe and well,' his mother refilled his cup.

'It was great to see Toome again. But, I soon found I was far from safe. People came after me because I'd been in the army. Being threatened be me own countrymen was a terrible setback – would me wars never end? Once frightened, you're always wary. I was on me guard constantly, I'd to learn who I could rely on. I got over it as best I could, kept me mouth shut and pretended to be stupid when it suited me. But, every election, I'm anxious again when candidates shout and get people worked up. Still fighting the civil war, still living in the past, no wonder the country's going nowhere. Last election, I had a rock thrown through the window, the hole's still there.

'There are times when I can't fight any longer. Particularly on nights when the wind howls or there's thunder and lightning. Then, it all comes back to me. The peals are the worst, it's like the war's started all over again. I've to get out, race away, otherwise me mind will go. You can see now why I don't talk about it too often.'

'Dan, the main thing is that you survived, you came back. Even though they may not tell you, many villagers admire you for what you have been through. Our door is open, you can talk to us anytime. Call up if you are stuck for a few eggs or a couple of shillings – as long as you do not spend it all in Mick FrenchShea's.'

'You don't miss a trick, mam,' he raised his cup. 'May you live as long as you want, and never want as long as you live.'

'Dan, you are one of the village's great characters, we would be lost without you,' his mother gathered up the cups.

'There's a few I couldn't keep up with, though,' Dan put on his cap.

'Will you ever forget Din Slattery returning from Blighty every year in his sunny Panama? Treating the whole village to drink and stories of his new life as a building contractor. It was only after he fell off scaffolding, that we discovered he laboured all year on the sites just to earn enough to make a splash in Toome. And little Mary Hayes, stepping off the bus in her high heels and the first pair of slacks ever seen in the village. Asking in a posh accent for directions to Bunacum, where she'd lived all her life. Neighbours laughed at her but didn't she and Din entertain us? Didn't they add a bit of colour to our lives? Where would we be without a bit of fantasy? Isn't that what lifts us, like your books and the plays and travelling shows?'

Toomevara was not short of characters. The children's favourite was Con Dermody. Every election, once candidates had departed, he would jump on the school wall and after promising 'Free Everything', would shower his audience with new pennies. Saddler Gordon Birch could be relied on for both farming intelligence and accurate weather forecasts. 'Did you hear the latest?' Molly Barney observed the street across her half-door and relayed parish news from early morning.

Farmer George Powell had followed every funeral for twenty years in his pony and trap. Retired labourer Din Ryan puffed the days away on his bull's-head pipe and blamed the new atom bomb for every storm. People came from miles to marvel at Big Jim O'Meara's card tricks. Carpenter Tommy the Timekeeper could not write but his waistcoat boasted two fountain pens, as well as an elaborate watch. A new table for Jim O'Meara proved too large to exit the door. Farmer Johnny Kennedy called after the shaft of his cart had broken. 'I'll make sure of the measurements first,' Tommy laid a length of timber on the good shaft and then sawed through both pieces of wood.

Paddy Dwyer was probably the most enterprising. One of the first to reach the site of the Blessed Virgin's appearance in the hills of Curraheen, he became friends with young Jimmy Walshe, who had witnessed the apparition. Paddy's regular attendance convinced pilgrims that he also had been visited by the Virgin. Donations for touching visitors' rosaries enabled him to fulfil his life-long dream of a silver watch. But when Mrs Tierney, who closed her shop promptly at six each evening, requested a hand on her beads, Paddy consulted his timepiece: 'Sorry, mam, no blessings after six.'

If Dan and he did not find the medals soon, they might have to seek Paddy's intercession. But, maybe not. The discovery of their miscalculation had boosted his confidence. He felt they were closing in on the long-lost biscuit tin. But he first had to convince the Gunner.

7.

Roses of Picardy

'Dan, you know I can't be seen talking to you.'

'Another great day, *marchons, marchons!*' the Gunner hoisted his crowbar on Friday morning. 'See you later, Salvo, drink your water.'

The sun dazzled them, as they ascended the slope. 'My mother says you do not walk as quickly as you used to, Dan.'

'The cheek of her, wait 'til she gets to my age. But it doesn't stop me climbing this hill – or getting out for a jar of an evening.'

'And, not for a long time to come, Dan. But your shorter steps these days means that our measurements were out again. The ten you took in the rath last week were not as long as those you measured the night you buried your medals.'

'Bejasus, you're your father's son all right, you don't miss a trick. Give me time to think about your plans. I was never good at the sums, where would that lave us now?'

They started five feet closer to the first of the hawthorns. The Gunner levered his way into the earth. 'A nice dry corner, it's not that hard.'

As Dan rested, he resumed shovelling. Easy at first, the dry soil soon became harder to excavate. Being close to the bigger trees meant that there were more roots. 'A bloody jungle, worse than Piccadilly Circus,' the Gunner looked around. 'But whatever we do, we mustn't damage the hawthorns.'

'Did you have a good time the other night, Dan?' he shovelled carefully.

'The news gets around here faster than the telegraph,' the Gunner paused.

'I met Paddy Galvin and Johnny Carroll and after putting the world to rights, we'd a bit of a sing-song. 'Twas like being back in the *estaminets* again. I gave them 'Mademoiselle from Armentières' and 'Roses of Picardy':

Roses are shining in Picardy, in the hush of
   the silver dew,
Roses are flowering in Picardy, but there's
   never a rose like you!
And the roses will die with the summertime,
   and our roads may be far apart,
But there's one rose that dies not in Picardy!
   'tis the rose that I keep in my heart!'

'Did you ever think of finding your own Rose,
Dan?'

The Gunner looked towards Grenanstown. 'At
school, one of me best friends was Jane O'Brien,
from just down the road there. She had long shiny
black hair and was ready for any mischief. We
picked blackberries and hazelnuts and fished in
the river and Boland's pond. I would sometimes
go back to her house after lessons. When we got
older, I often spoke to her in the village. One of
the best nights of me life was when I was eighteen and we went to a ceilidh at Ballinamona. We
danced the whole night together. She told me that
if I bought a gramophone, she'd marry me and
then we could dance for the rest of our lives.'

Dan sighed and ran a hand across his face.
'But, then, the war distracted me and that was
that. When I came home, her parents didn't want
her to see me, because I'd been in the army. I
think they'd been warned off. One morning, she

smiled across the street at me from Looby's shop. I hopped over on the double. "Dan, you know I can't be seen talking to you," she rushed inside.

'A couple of years after we got our own government, she took the mailboat to Holyhead, a long way from Ballinamona. I often thought about her and hoped she would come back. But, like so many schoolmates, I never saw her again. I heard she became a nurse. There's more village people now in Birmingham and Coventry than there are here at home. Including, can you credit it, Jack Hourican's own children. They'd all be still here if he and diehards like him had waited for Home Rule instead of killing people and ruining the country.'

'But, would you not like to be married and have someone to look after you?'

'Looked after? You mean be told what to do for the rest of me life,' the Gunner looked at him.

'Like poor Dick Brady, a prisoner in his own home, he can't even get out for a pint anymore. Or Johnnie Cody with six mouths to feed and they all walking barefoot to school. Or Paddy Johnson, whose wife left him a week after they married. "Neither of us is who we thought we were," she skipped back to her parents.

'People feel sorry for me because I've neither wife nor money. But, after being a number and told what to do for four long year, I now enjoy being me own boss. I can get up when I want to, go to bed when I like. He travels fastest who travels alone. And when I get a bit of work, I've enough shillings to get on with, and no one telling me how to spend it. I can have all the company and fun a man could ever want in a choice of snug pubs.'

Removing the clay demanded patience. Every time he filled the spade, half of it fell back as he navigated a root. By midday, the hole was only half the length they had excavated the first days. 'Hard going. But better slow work in the right place – assuming that's where we are – than faster in the wrong one,' Dan led him downhill.

In the distance, a car revved loudly. 'Father Cosgrave attacking Lisatoggart hill again,' Dan looked westwards. 'Tipp's worst driver, wouldn't you feel sorry for the poor Baby Ford?'

They dug to the right of the trench when they resumed after lunch. With fewer obstructions, they made better progress. By three they had matched their morning efforts.

'There might be something here,' the Gunner levered carefully.

'Springy and soft, it feels like a root. But it's not. It's never me biscuit tin, is it?' he flung down the crowbar. 'Give me the spade, quick.'

'You are like a dog unearthing a bone, Dan,' he stood back, as clay flew in all directions.

The Gunner stopped digging and reached down. He tugged until the object was free. He was right, it was not a root. And neither was it his long-buried tin. It was a triangle of leather.

'How the hell could a piece of harness get up here?' he flung it to the ground. 'I thought we were in business there for a minute.

'But I think we've solved a village mystery,' he laughed. 'This is where Tommy Barney's ass must have hidden after her halter broke and she ran away one evening years ago. Tommy searched everywhere, but it wasn't until the following morning that she was found looking over the gate down there beside the road. She must have hidden in the rath, this must be the remains of the halter.'

Though disappointed, the boy was encouraged at the same time. The find strengthened his belief that their hard work and plans would lead them to the medals. More excitement was to follow. As they resumed work, the Gunner suddenly grabbed his arm. 'Sh, shush. Someone's coming up the hill.'

They both stood still, the voices came closer. 'We'll head them off at the pass,' Dan lurched to the pile of stones the children had discarded. He picked up four or five, flung them into the hole and grabbed his crowbar.

A hurley parted the furze, Jim Hickey and John Joe McCormack walked in. 'Well, the divil take youse, you gave me an awful start,' Dan pretended to drop the bar in fright.

'You're mining for gold?' they looked into the trench.

'I wish, a nugget or two would go a long way in FrenchSheas,' Dan retrieved the bar.

'I'm extending me little garden and those fellows down there are just the things to enclose it,' he picked up two of the stones and carried them back to the heap. 'What do you think of that pile so far?'

'No better man for the horticulture, you'll be exhibiting at Nenagh Show next with Gordon Birch,' Jim thumped him on the back, before he and John Joe resumed their way to Carroll's field to practise.

'You have not forgotten how to duck and dive,' he complimented Dan.

'You'd have to get up early in the morning to catch the Gunner out. But, we must keep our little secret to ourselves. Then everyone will have an even bigger surprise when we strike it rich.'

They worked for another half an hour before the Gunner said it was time for home. He seemed disappointed. 'Do not worry, Dan. As long as we are digging, we are making progress. We will keep going until we find your treasure,' he started to fill in the trench.

The sound of the men coming up the hill had startled the Gunner. It had reminded him of the night he'd buried his medals. Glancing over his shoulder every minute, to see if anyone was tracking him. He looked down and shuddered. He thought of Paddy Smith dumped one dark night into a hole like that. Without respect or any friend to comfort him. 'What's that you said?' he asked the boy.

'I was saying that the more we search, the closer we are to finding them.'

'You're right, Sherlock. We may not know where they are but we now know where they're not. Don't be upset, I still think it's hard graft and not penmanship that will find me medals.'

'You are a hard man to persuade, Dan,' the boy checked his boots before heading home.

The evening breeze eddied the dust as he walked. It also fanned his concerns. As well as the Gunner, he had his mother to contend with. He knew he could not fool her forever. Keeping secrets and getting bigger was more complicated than he had thought. As was the discovery that things were not always as he had been led to believe, and that people could hold such different opinions. He would have to adapt and learn new skills. A pity that among all its treasures, the fortnightly library offered nothing to which he could turn for practical advice. He would probably have to learn the hard way, which the Gunner always insisted was the only way.

In bed that night, he accepted that it would be impossible for anyone to have complete recall after thirty years. And, particularly, someone like the war-damaged Gunner. But, there was no doubting Dan's vivid memory of the frights he had experienced inside the rath. The rustling noise and his shadow on those stones were still very real to him. The stones! Surely these were the key to their quest? Why had he not thought of this before? If only he could pinpoint their original location, they must have left some trace?

There was one other thing he should investigate. What if the Gunner had made a mistake about the position of his shadow? That was easier to check. As they were digging at the same time of the year that the Gunner had hidden his medals, the moon should now be in exactly the same place. Though it was a bright evening, he saw its outline at half past eight over Boland's mill. Looking out his bedroom window two hours later, it lit up the barracks and the Nenagh road. By midnight, at the time the Gunner had buried his treasure, it would have moved to the west. The Gunner's shadow would have been on his right, as he had always insisted.

Relieved at this assurance, he fell asleep to the *krek krek* of the riverside corncrakes. He remembered the Gunner one morning reciting a poem about the river to his mother:

> 'I chatter over stony ways,
> In little sharps and trebles,
> I bubble into eddying bays,
> I babble on the pebbles.

'A soothing retreat, mam, is there anything as calming as a river? You hear of those rich ladies above in Dublin splashing out on medicines and massages to cool their nerves. If they sat on that bridge for five minutes, the splashing of the water would soon wash away all their troubles – and save them a fortune. And the river's always merry and bright. Never the same note, like those bells you'd hear from the grand churches.'

' "There's no money in water, Dan," young Jim O'Meara stopped one morning as I was sitting there.

'He laughed when I told him it was for me health and that it would do him and the other merchants good to sit down too and relax. But they race hither and thither, trying to make an extra penny or outsmart someone less sharp than themselves. And for what, they can't take it with them when Your Man Above calls? And all their talk about eternity, when it's right in front of their eyes to be enjoyed. Nature, the real eternity. Here for everyone from prince to pauper, am I not right, mam? If I'd me way, I'd bring all the generals and all the Kaisers here and get them to pow-wow around the river. They'd soon realise how wonderful it was to be alive and well and concentrate on enjoying life, not destroying it.'

There was no digging next day. The Gunner was doing his fortnightly cleaning of the barracks, a job his father had given him many years before. As the boy sat on the garden seat, he remembered the excitement the Gunner and he had shared a few weeks earlier, when Circuit of Ireland rally competitors had roared into the village and stopped around Casey's garage. He had never heard so many different accents. Nor seen such colourful and sporty cars, many with their hoods down. Ruby Austins and Humbers, sleek white-numbered Jaguars and red and blue MGs.

'After the travelling shows, the most exciting thing we've seen in Toome,' the Gunner limped around the vehicles.

'A lovely machine, what will she do, sir?' he asked the moustachioed driver of a green wire-wheeled Singer.

'With a following gale, around seventy,' the Englishman's shoulders went up and down.

'Over a mile a minute, I wish we'd something like her when we were sending back for supplies at Mons.'

'You were at Mons in 1914?'

'With the Royal Munsters. I was there for so long, I'd begun to think we were the Royal French.'

'Well, I'll be damned,' the man removed his driving gloves.

'Major Robin Rhodes, retired. I was just up the road from you with the Glosters. How we both had our noses bloodied that August. Hundreds killed, missing. But you chaps covered our retreat until your ammo ran out. You held off five times your numbers for over a day. Thanks to you, we turned things around at the Marne. We still talk about it. Steady the Buffs. This calls for a celebration.'

'Gunner Daniel Doherty at your service. You're the first fellow-soldier I've met since I came home thirty year ago,' Dan saluted.

'Only a few of us left,' the Major opened O'Meara's door.

The two of them were singing when they emerged from the pub:

'We beat 'em on the Marne,
We beat 'em on the Aisne,
They gave us hell at Neuve Chapelle
But here we are again.'

His slouch was gone, the Gunner seemed eight feet tall. 'An honour to meet a Munster,' the Major extended his hand. 'It was you and your mates Marshal Foch was talking about when he said that France would never forget her debt to the heroic Irish.

'Now, give me your address and I'll drop you a line from Bristol,' he produced his route-book.

'This is my secretary, a much better writer than me,' the Gunner handed the book to the boy.

'The world's youngest aide-de-camp. Quality must be rewarded, have a mineral,' the Major handed him a florin – enough for eight lemonades. 'But, learn from Dan and myself. Wars damage your health, give them a wide berth. Be a good aide and look after this man. He is a hero. Without him and his pals, I might not be alive.'

'*Bon Voyage*,' the Gunner shut the door of the Singer. '*Ils ne passeront pas!*'

'They shall not pass, indeed. *Salut*, see you next year,' the Major raised his hand. 'Then, maybe, we will pay our respects at the Modreeny grave of fellow-Mons man and Victoria Cross winner, James Somers. And afterwards drive to Templemore, to see padre Francis Gleeson's home. On my wall, I have the famous picture of him blessing you Munsters at Rue du Bois.'

He was pleased for the Gunner, that he had finally met someone who shared his experiences, that his contribution had been acknowledged. But, how different Dan's life was to the Major's. Had he been born in England, he might own a Singer too, instead of existing on a small pension. He would also have treatment for his injuries. And why indeed in his own village, did some people own so much? While those who worked for them had so little and less chance of education or advancement. Molly Barney interrupted his thoughts. 'How did the Gunner know that man?'

'They fought together during the war, the Major said he was a hero who saved many lives.'

'Well, fancy that,' Molly hastened across the road to Mrs Tierney.

The Gunner and he waved goodbye as the Major sped away. The Singer and the other cars raised a cloud of dust as they raced down the Silvermines road. How he wished he could travel with them. He clung to the sound of the engine notes, until they faded away behind the hills.

Soon, they would be on the other side of Keeper. The village reverted to silence again. He thought there was a tear in Dan's eye, as he relit his pipe and murmured 'That was a mighty surprise, a voice from the past.'

He was as excited as the Gunner. The rally broadcast an exotic outside world. As did his parents' wireless, from which strange accents and wavering music connected him with London, Paris and Hilversum. Their *Cassells Books of Knowledge* displayed photos of wondrous scenery and buildings even further afield. And sights he could not have imagined. Boats sailing through the streets of Venice, oranges growing on Spanish sidewalks. How exciting it would be to see those places. How he would love to wander the Silk Road in Marco Polo's footsteps. But, his parents could never afford to travel, how could he, even when he was bigger? He still hoped he would. He remembered the Gunner's advice, 'If you dream, you're half way there.'

He looked down towards the barracks. The Gunner was just finishing the bottom windows. He went back to his own work and the sketch of the rath. Were they digging anywhere near the right place? That clay pipe was all they had to show for four days' toil. He thought again about the stones. He imagined the children removing them to build their house. And how bare the ground would have looked without them. Just like the pale patches left on the grass when the travelling shows unpegged their tents and departed the village square. Suddenly, he remembered the Gunner's history lesson and what he had said about the flying archaeologists. How they had traced long-hidden sites by observing the ground from above. He might not have an aeroplane but surely he might gain a similar aspect from the heights of his favourite tree?

8.

A Vital Clue

'Maybe, tomorrow will be the big day?'

A day of rest, he could do all the climbing he wanted on Sunday afternoon. But, first, he had to get permission to go to the rath. His mother was in a good mood. She was going to visit Hannah and Maggie, the widowed sisters who lived across the street in Looby's shop. She would be there for at least a couple of hours, as they reminisced around the Aga cooker. 'The Gunner is gone away for the day. But is it all right if I go and play for a while on the hill by myself? Then, I will come home and study,' he placed his schoolbooks on the table.

'Off you go then,' she put on her coat. 'But change out of your good clothes first.'

He accelerated across the bridge, assailed by additional Sabbath guilt about his secret. He was looking forward to tackling the oak again. Adventure and a challenge, his own boss, he felt alive when he climbed.

Ascending to a different world, a secret hideaway remote from everything below. And what a lively universe it hosted. Insects criss-crossing the branches, thrushes and finches warbling non-stop, sparrows squabbling underneath. His mother did not like him climbing but for him, the tree had always been a friendly sanctuary. And he saw it in a different light, since the Gunner and he had stood underneath it on the first day of his holidays. 'You're connecting with nature, when you climb one. But don't tell herself I said that,' Dan had patted the oak.

'Trees are living beings just like us. Look at those branches celebrating life, like children flying in all directions. Providing homes for the birds, painting the countryside so green in summer and red and golden brown in autumn. Do you know they give out the oxygen which keeps us all alive? And, fifty foot high, this fella lifts our thoughts towards the heavens just like those cathedrals. Little wonder it's regarded as the king of trees. The ancient Druids worshipped under it, the Christians after them, the name of Kildare is taken from St. Brigid's oak church. As a poem I learned at school went:

> The oak it is a noble tree,
> The monarch of the wood;
> Through winter's storms a thousand years,
> Its hardy trunk hath stood.

'And none better for solid wood. The decks of the most famous boats from the Viking invaders to Nelson's fleet were all oak. Down through the years, builders have used it for house beams, winemakers for their barrels. And it makes the best furniture. When it eventually falls, this tree will continue to live even longer in someone's front room. A hundred year old, it will still be here, when we're long gone.'

The oak's height was intimidating, but its leaves waved an irresistible invitation. He removed his boots and socks, bare feet would be best for the fissured bark. He climbed easily to the second branch and looked down. From fifteen feet, the rath floor seemed much the same as it did at ground level. He focused his gaze and thought he detected a circular image near where the Gunner said the stones had been. Maybe, this was just because he had wanted to see something?

He decided to go to the next branch, as high as he had ever climbed before. He scanned the entire area before returning to the area directly underneath. The discolouration seemed more pronounced, a lighter patch in its dark surroundings. He was still uncertain. The only way to find out was to ascend even higher. If he fell, there would be no one to help him. Should he go back down and wait until tomorrow when the Gunner was there? But, remembering his mother's warnings about climbing, he knew that Dan would never allow him.

He clasped the grey trunk, stretched his arms and hauled himself upwards. The additional grip inspired confidence, he had been right to remove his footwear. The branch swayed, would it be strong enough to support him? His apprehension increased as he saw how high he was. He tightened his hold on the trunk before finally concluding he was safe. It was the furthest he had ever climbed, he felt achieved. He looked down. And, this time, there was no doubt. A circle of about two feet in diameter stood out from the rest of the ground, this must be the place where the heap of stones had stood. It was about twenty feet from two large hawthorns to its left. Could one of these be the young tree the Gunner had first observed?

He wished he had something to drop down as a marker. He memorised the nearest hollows and shrubs, before lowering himself carefully to the branch below. And then, more surely to solid ground. He went to the stones the children had taken and placed one in the centre of where he was now sure the pile had originally stood. They would dig there tomorrow and if they found any similar rocks, they would know that this was the site of the shadow which had so frightened the Gunner. Excavating in straight lines between the marker and each of the hawthorns, they should soon locate their treasure.

'How can you smile so early on a Monday morning?' Dan emerged from his house. 'Did you win the Sweepstakes draw?'

'I found something even better than the Sweep,' he produced his latest sketch.

'Not another bloody map? You remind me of those Generals scheming up new Fronts though at least, unlike them, you're in the lines with me.'

Would he ever convince the Gunner? 'Do you remember, Dan, what you told me about Bill O'Meara and the archaeologists? How they could find hidden sites by examining the ground from the air.'

'Those fellas had aeroplanes,' the Gunner pushed back his cap.

'No plane yet, Dan, but if they could see from up high, so can I. That is what I did yesterday, when you were away.'

'Up in the trees again. If your mother finds out, we're both done for. Tell me more.'

He explained what he had observed from his vantage point. 'The fellas who dug up Tutankhamun didn't go to so much trouble,' Dan restored his cap. 'The stones place is long covered and you know what I think of your plans. But – there's one born every day – I'll go up with you anyhow for another look.'

He showed Dan the stone which he hoped marked the location of the original pile.

'I'm afraid I can't see anything different from the rest of the ground,' the Gunner circled. 'And we still have the problem of deciding which of those hawthorns is the young one I saw all those years ago. Each is about the same distance I paced out from the rocks, about twenty foot. But they're twelve foot apart and they both look exactly the same.'

'No problem, Dan,' he produced his plan, on which he had drawn a triangle from the site of the heap to each of the hawthorns.

'We will search along the top line first and, then, the other. And if neither produces anything, we will dig in between. That way, the whole area will be covered. If I am correct about where the red stones were, we will be on the right track. The children could not have taken all of them, they must have left one or two. If we find a similar one, we will know we are closing in on your treasure.'

'You'd sell fridges to the Eskimos, off you go with the spade.'

He put the marker rock to one side. The bees swarmed around the hawthorns' white blossoms, he could smell the musky scent.

'If we could harness those fellas, we'd have the whole place dug within a day. Aren't we blessed with the weather again?' the Gunner took over.

Whenever Dan rested, he removed the clay. Soon they were a foot down. If there was anything there, surely they should have found it by now?

'My turn,' the Gunner resumed.

He swivelled from side to side. 'I think I've hit something solid, off you go with your spade.'

He removed a layer of soil. A few inches down, he reached the top of the object. It was a stone all right, one of the biggest they had encountered.

Could it be one that had proved too heavy for the children to move? He cleared away some more earth, put the spade aside and bent down. Stretching underneath the rock, he lifted it up with both hands. It was large and triangular. He scraped off the clinging clay. The colour was reddish-brown, exactly like those the young housebuilders had used. Looking down into the hole, he saw a similar stone.

'Full marks, you're a genius, that's where the heap was all right,' Dan waved the crowbar. 'Maybe the pen is mightier than the spade after all? Count me in, I'll go along with your plans from now on. Like that harvesting, cooperation's the secret of success, I should follow me own advice. The excitement's getting too much for me. Let's have a break to cool down.'

'I have witnessed a miracle,' the boy laid his spade aside and followed Dan down the hill.

'What a pity you can't tell your mother,' the Gunner called back.

Salvo observed them as they drank their tea. 'Look,' Dan held his cup in mid-air. 'He's now putting weight on the bad leg. Our hard work's paying off on all fronts. Well done, me little redbreast.'

When they resumed work, the Gunner scraped out two lines in the ground, just as he

112

had pencilled on his map. They started half way across the upper track. It was slow going. The multitude of roots included some thicker ones from the oak. 'No wonder it's stayed up there all these years', Dan ran his shirt sleeve across his forehead.

By the time they broke at midday, they had managed to get down to the depth of the Gunner's hiding place. But their excavation was only two feet wide. After lunch, he took over Dan's crowbar. They toiled for an hour and a half and broadened the trench around the target area. He had hoped they would have found something by now, but he had to accept they would have to wait until tomorrow. 'Bloody roots, I'm a bit tired, we'll finish early and have a cuppa before you head home', the Gunner picked up the bar.

'We are going in the right direction, Dan', he brushed his boots. 'Maybe, tomorrow will be the big day?'

'Talking about those archaeological aeroplanes, did I ever tell you of the machines that were shot down near me during the war?' the Gunner sat down beside him on the grass.

'On the odd days when the Generals decided who to kill somewhere else, we diverted ourselves be studying dogfights in the air above. The drone of the engines was music after the thunder of artillery. The manoeuvring was like the tag we played outside Toome school, everyone wheeling and swerving to avoid being caught. With the grey machines so high up, it was only when the cannons flashed that you realised there were human beings like ourselves inside.

'One late summer morning, we watched a Hun and one of our own go after each other. They ducked and dived and twirled their biplanes right over, like the swallows racing around the village. It looked as if the enemy had the better of it, until our fella came up behind him and let loose. The German was hit and lost control. But what happened but didn't his plane drop on top of the man who'd just shot him. The machines tangled and started falling together. Round and round they went. One minute we were looking at the black German cross, then the red, white and blue RAF roundel. They gathered speed and smashed into the ground a couple of hundred yards from us.

'We raced across to the wreckage. The German, a lad about twenty-five, was lying back, dead, blood trickling out of his mouth. Our man hadn't a scratch but his head was hanging sideways, he'd broken his neck. I'd seen many killed before, but to see these two at close quarters gave me a terrible start. Both around the same age, they could have been twins. You couldn't have told them apart but for their khaki and grey-green uniforms. I helped pull them out and lay them on the ground. They were as warm as if they were still alive. We went through their pockets and found their photos. Dieter from Wiesbaden with his wife and young daughter. Our Oswald smiling on his own Scarborough wedding day only three months earlier.

'Looking at them lying on the wasteland around us, I'm not ashamed to tell you, the tears rolled down me eyes. Those lads would never see their homes or families again. It was then that it struck me. All the fighting and bloody killing was nothing less than a crime. And as stupid as it was unnecessary. Dieter was just as human as ourselves. Like us, he probably hadn't wanted to go to war. I could never hate him nor his comrades again. That was the day me war ended. And with it, me belief in fighting for country and all the rest we were told be leaders, who stayed well away from the battlefield. I'd never again fall for that guff.

'I fired into the air from then on, not across at the enemy. Lucky for me, the armistice was soon signed before I was found out. That was me best day of the war. The eleventh hour of the eleventh month, 1918. I'll never forget it,' Dan drained his mug.

'Freed from the prison of the trenches, we all stood on open ground for the first time in years. It was great to breathe fresh air again. We heard a bird singing somewhere. A blackbird, can you imagine? For a minute I thought I was back on me own little hill. Suddenly, fellas started to run, do cartwheels and punch each other on the back. "Back to Blighty, we're going home, we're going home!" they shouted.

'Helmets flew in the air, rum was passed around. Someone produced a mouthorgan. Soon everyone, even officers, were dancing with each other. And those who didn't dance sang "Mademoiselle from Armentieres" and "Pack up Your Troubles in Your Old Kit Bag". I thought of Jane when they all belted out:

> "It's a long way to Tipperary,
> It's a long way to go.
> It's a long way to Tipperary
> And the sweetest girl I know!"

'There was a spring in our step as we headed home. But each mile through a wasteland of wrecked tanks and tree stumps was a reminder of what the French and Belgians had endured. Not a trace left of the orchards, corn-ricks or lovely flower gardens we'd seen four year earlier. Even the graveyards had been torn up. A few leaning gables were all that stood of the buildings we'd admired. Arras was flattened, its cathedral reduced to a shell. Where was our God when all this happened?

'As we marched, ragged children and old people appeared from nowhere. We gave them some of our rations, as they scavenged for anything they could get their hands on. The roads were packed with civilian survivors struggling back to see what was left of their homes. There were no young men. An old woman, little more than a bag of bones, was being pushed over the potholes in a wooden wheelbarrow. 'Twould melt the heart of a stone. How would she and they ever pick up their lives again?

'But, coming through what was left of one village, I heard the sound of water above the marching feet. I couldn't believe it. A fountain, half blown away, still working. I ran me hand through the flow. It was like I was baptised again. As if I was starting a second existence. A chance not many get. I couldn't wait to get home, and begin to live again. But I was sorry to leave me mates, I knew I'd hardly ever see them again. "*Slan libh*," I waved goodbye to them as I trundled out of London.'

' "*Pog mo thoin*," they shouted back.

'They hadn't forgotten the rude words of Irish I'd taught them.'

The boy could hardly sleep that night, thinking of what the Gunner had told him. How terrible that those fliers had been killed. And so young - and for what? He was beginning to think, like the Gunner, that war was the biggest evil on earth, not all the other things the Missions priests preached about. He had never once heard them condemn war. No more than the politicians, who celebrated conflict as they shouted from the school wall about the great fight for Irish freedom. He too would have to be careful not to be taken in by such people.

His admiration for the Gunner increased, Dan's belief in his plans energised him. Tomorrow, he would work even harder to help him. Tomorrow should provide their best chance of finding the long-lost medals. But what condition would they be in after so long underground?

9.

The Gunner's Migraine

'When I'm better, I'll thank you for teaching me the value of good health.'

'That man must be going to plant an awful lot of turnips. The pair of you have been seen digging up there, that explains your dirty shoes,' his mother saw him off on Tuesday morning.

'We will have to go down next week and see what you are up to. Mrs Tierney heard Dan saved a lot of lives in France, ask him to tell us more next time he is here.'

Was his mother finally getting suspicious? They would have to find the medals soon. The Gunner was not at the door to greet him, he had

119

to knock. 'Not so loud,' he emerged, rubbing his eyes.

'This could be our big day, Dan. Your memory is much better than you thought. Locating the stones proved that. All we have to do now is work along the lines and we will be in business.'

The Gunner seemed quiet. 'I'm right behind you,' he gasped, as they approached the rath.

Preparing to dig, he could see that Dan was not his usual self. He staggered and kept closing and opening his eyes. As he started to work, he nearly stabbed himself in the foot with his crowbar.

'Were you out last night, Dan?'

'I wish I had been,' the Gunner sat down.

'The head's killing me. And the light. I'm afraid I'm coming down with one of me migraines. They're a bloody nightmare, I've had them since the war. They come and go but when they arrive, they knock me out completely. I'm sorry, we'll have to postpone the work. Will you ask Doc Murphy to come down and see me? He'll put me right. Then, the sooner I'm better, the quicker we get back to business. We'll start in two or three days again and then, with your plan, I'm sure we'll finally strike it lucky.'

From anticipation to disappointment, he was taken aback by this sudden change of events. They were now so close to success, he had thought today might be the big day. But what was his upset compared to the Gunner's distress? The man was even shaking. It was time he learned some patience. 'No problem, Dan. I will carry everything down,' he shouldered his spade and trailed the heavier crowbar behind him.

'And I wasn't able to get out for milk this morning,' Dan reached for the door latch.

'I'll go up to Harty's for you. Would you like me to get some tobacco as well?'

'An ounce of St Bruno would save me life. Ask Jack to put it on the slate, I'll fix up as soon as I'm out and about.'

Shy to ask the shopkeeper for credit, the boy remembered the Major's two shillings. What better way to spend them than on the Major's comrade? He ran home with the milk can and collected the florin. As he paid Jack, he noticed the display tin of fig-rolls. Dan did not enjoy many luxuries. 'Could I have threepence worth of those as well?' he asked.

'Your milk and baccy and and some afters,' he handed over the shopping. 'And, no slate to worry about. I used the Major's money – and I still have the price of three lemonades.'

'A terrible lad, you're taking after the mother, but I'll make it up to you one day,' Dan seized his hand.

Putting the unexpected free time to good use, he studied his latest map to see if there was anything he could add. He rechecked all the lines and measurements and was satisfied that he had done the best job. He was confident they would find the medals. Missing the *Biggles* volume down the side of the armchair, his mother was pleasantly surprised to find him poring over his books. 'I see you cannot wait to go up the hill again,' she interrupted his study of Ireland's geography.

        ℞   ℞   ℞

'Bloody migraines, I've got over most things but I can't avoid you,' the Gunner seesawed in his bed down the Silvermines road. 'We're like an ould married couple, I probably wouldn't know meself without you.'

He shifted position to reduce the pain. 'But I'll survive you, like I've learned to survive everything else. If I hadn't, who else would have done it for me? Sixteen million died, I escaped, wasn't I the lucky soldier? I can see and hear, I only got a touch of the gaz. Do your worst, but I'll send you packing too. And, when I'm better, I'll thank you for teaching me the value of good health.'

The regular visitation was another price he was still paying for the war. Maybe, he should never have left Toome? If he'd stayed, Jane might be beside him now. But it had been his only chance to explore, to escape an endless future of labouring. If he hadn't signed up, he wouldn't have seen or learned so much. He'd experienced the wonder of distant countries, the stimulation of new friendships. And four years of bully beef and winters caked in mud had educated him on the idiocy of jingoism, the gullibility of man.

He had acquired fresh values, a more informed appreciation of what was important in life. The depths his species could reach. Squandering millions on destruction that would have saved everyone from the Spanish Flu. And the heights. It wasn't for him to tell anyone what to believe in, we all find our own gods. But he would never forget his last sight of Padre Henshaw. Crucifix in hand, striding into no-man's land to help a crying soldier. And, then, the sniper's volley that cut him down too. 'I'd say 'twas all worth it,' he forced a smile and turned again in his bed.

The war – and the fear on his return – had been nightmares. But, far from greed and pettiness, how encouraging the trench companionship had been. As long as he lived, he would remember the chaplain and all his fallen comrades:

They shall not grow old, as we that are
   left grow old:
Age shall not weary them, nor the years
   condemn.
At the going down of the sun and in the
   morning,
We will remember them...

He had thought it a great joke when villag-ers laughed at the idea of gold above in the rath. He was the only one who knew there was. And treasure that was even more valuable to him than gold. But the joke was really on him. Why hadn't he continued searching until he found his med-als, instead of leaving them to rot in the damp ground? Why hadn't he got someone to help him earlier? But if they'd told his visitors, he'd have been a dead man, particularly when they heard how he'd tricked them.

It had been a challenge, but patience had finally paid off. He wished he could have found the medals himself. But he shouldn't be ashamed that he'd come to depend on the boy. Hadn't the war been teamwork as well? Trusting the boy with his story had been like the relief of a siege, what encouragement and bright company he'd provided. One of the few who'd shown any interest in his experiences, he regularly asked about Amiens and other places in which he had soldiered. When he said he would do something, he did. And what a thorough young man, with his sketches and plans.

He envied the boy's youth and enthusiasm. He was happy to think that, with his schooling, he would never have to enlist to earn a few bob. His curiosity and sense of adventure reminded him of his distant youth. A lad after his own heart, he felt he would live on in him. The boy believed in the search, and so did he. The digging was like his battle to survive. If you sat back, you fell down. He hadn't given up that day in no man's land, he wouldn't give up now. Once better, he'd be up the hill again. And they'd find his medals. 'Stick that in your pipe, Mr Migraine, and smoke it.'

❧   ❧   ❧

Two days later, the Gunner called to the boy's house. 'Great to see you about again, Dan,' his mother answered the door.

'Hard to kill a bad thing,' he doffed his cap.

'And you never lost your timing, the kettle has just boiled. Sit down and to help you recover, a scone hot from the oven.'

'God bless you, mam, you're as good as the doc.'

'Do you often get the headaches, Dan?'

'I've had them for years. Like the nightmares, it was the bombardments that started them,' he reached for the jam.

'I'll tell you but no one else, I relive the war many nights. I can still hear me first shell, screaming towards us like a supersonic banshee. Where would it hit? There was a big crash, the ground shook. Muck and rocks everywhere, it left a hole the size of this room. Another twenty yards, I'd have been a gonner. I couldn't hear or think straight for days. I shook for as many and remembering it is nearly as bad. That's why I keep it all to meself and why, I suppose, I run around some nights.'

'There were a few who never heard the sound of a shell but who did well out of them,' his father interrupted.

'You never said a truer word, Sergeant,' Dan's cup clattered against its saucer.

'The worst villains of the lot, how could anyone forgive the arms makers? If it wasn't for them, I wouldn't have me headaches and all me poor pals would still be alive. They lived in style far away from the fighting and well rewarded they were. Albert Vickers decorated, Machine Gun Maxim made a Sir. Those scoundrels never got trench feet or a whiff of gaz, but they made millions. One of them bought a big house down in

Cork and no one here said boo, the government nor anyone else.

'And I'm afraid, mam, the church doesn't come out of it well either. The bishops blessed us and told we were going off to defend Catholic Belgium. Cardinals on all sides holy-watered the battleships and tanks. We're told we're civilised, I think we've a long way to go. God forgive me, but I sometimes wonder if Himself Above isn't a bit of a comedian, that he put us down here just to entertain himself.'

He was surprised to hear his religious mother laugh. 'Dan, you are becoming a terrible infidel, but I have to agree with you. People often follow the loudest voice, gumption flies out the window.'

'You're right there. Throw in a few flags, a brass band, some nice uniforms and you're on a winner. Is there anything more lunatic than great nations putting all their energy and resources into slaughtering each other to a standstill? You couldn't invent it. Do you think we'll ever get sense – or will we just destroy the whole caboodle? Will it take a plague from outer space to bring us all to our senses?'

'Rome was not built in a day, Dan. It is misunderstanding and lack of communication that lead to war. Leaders are now finally learning to settle disputes by discussion, they are planning a European parliament. Imagine France, Germany and Britain debating peacefully in the one place, there would hardly ever be war again.'

'Well, the sooner the better, you've bucked me up again, mam. I sometimes think women are a step ahead of the men - and 'tis they who pick up the pieces after all the wars. You're right, debate's the only way. But, after two skirmishes in me life-time, I think it's a delicate plant which will have to be as regularly nourished as your flowers. A great help to get all that out of the system, but we won't talk about the war or the bad things from now on. I hope himself is free to come down again tomorrow.'

'No problem, Dan. He has been very good lately, the exercise is sharpening him up. He stud-ied over the past couple of days and even helped his father with the vegetable drills. But I still have to find out what you are up to in the rath. Maybe you are after treasure and hiding it all from me? I will have to go down for that inspection.'

'How did you find out, mam, 'twas supposed to be only between himself and meself?' the Gun-ner pulled the cap down over his forehead.

'We haven't found anything yet but, maybe, very soon. And you and the Sergeant will be the first to know.'

10.

The Gunner Becomes a Celebrity

*He knelt down so quickly, his cap fell
into the hole*

'Not a cloud in the sky, another grand day for it,' Dan looked around, as they climbed the hill on Friday morning.

'But, the red sky this morning is the shepherd's warning, it might rain later. The sooner we finish that first line, the sooner we can start on its neighbour. I was thinking about your plan last night. The more I thought about it, the more I felt you're on the right track. You're a clever young man. Brains and brawn, a great combination. We'll soon know, one way or the other.'

They agreed to extend the top-line excavation in each direction, before tackling the second. With the multitude of roots, the work proved more difficult than they had anticipated. 'But we must go slowly,' Dan levered carefully. 'These are the lads that feed our friends the trees.'

In two hours, they had extended the hole by only the same number of feet. 'No point in killing ourselves,' Dan downed his crowbar. 'We'll get our strength back with something sugared and hot.'

The robin was at the door when they arrived. 'Sharp as a razor, that fella always knows when it's taytime,' Dan brought out a piece of bread.

'Wouldn't it do your heart good to see him standing on both pins again? He'll soon be off gallivanting with his pals. Make sure you come back and see me, Salvo,' he threw the bread-crumbs.

As they sipped by the gable wall, the Gunner pointed to his little garden. 'We're killing ourselves looking for treasure but there's a trove right in front of our very eyes. Those foxgloves standing to attention, the wallflowers parading in front of them. The butterflies flitting from one to the other. Your parents should get a medal for their front garden. Like an oasis, it lifts the whole village. And look at those daisies and buttercups, arriving every year like Mrs Tierney's new carpets. Bright chains for the girls, a lively covering for the boys to tumble on.

'One of me favourites is lavender which I first saw in France, I'll never forget its lovely perfume. And the poppy. When we were marching up to Belgium, tired and not in our right minds, clusters of them lit up the corners of cratered fields. As we watched them waving in the evening breeze, Liverpool Pat, as fatigued and dusty as meself, tapped me shoulder "There's still hope for the world, Dan."

'Me only worry now is that those new chemicals may destroy a lot of them – and the butterflies. The planet's for the plants and birds and animals, as well as for ourselves. We should think twice before we interfere with nature.'

Occasionally swopping roles, they resumed their joust with the roots. Despite their best efforts, it was slow progress. By midday, the hole was four feet long, but they had found nothing. The Gunner leaned against his crowbar, as the more daring of a pair of thrushes alighted on the freshly-upturned soil. 'This ould digging's harder than I thought. If I only knew which of those hawthorns was the young one I saw, we might be home and dry now.'

'Do not worry, Dan. We have not wasted our time. We have eliminated one place, and digging the lower line should be much easier. If you look along to the other hawthorn, there are not half as many roots. We will start in the centre and be down a couple of feet in no time.'

'You're a great optimist, 'tis wonderful to be young,' the Gunner saw him off to the road.

He was disappointed for Dan that they had not found the medals. But, walking home for lunch, he was happy that they were now on the right track. He had faith in his plan, he could not wait to get started in the afternoon.

They commenced along the lower line, close to one of the hollows of the Gunner's earlier excavations. 'You first, President,' the Gunner handed him the spade.

The going was easier. 'You were right,' Dan leaned on his crowbar. 'No more roots or rocks.'

With the threat of rain, they worked harder. The earth quickly piled up. 'We spoke too early about the stones, will you shovel them up for me,' the Gunner rested the crowbar.

'There's only a couple of small ones, Dan,' he lifted them out.

It was then that he noticed what appeared to be a piece of cloth. He bent down for a closer look. It was like the oil tablecloth his mother had in the pantry. Could this be what they had worked so hard for? The Gunner's long-lost medals at last? As the Gunner had buried them, he should be the first to see them. 'You dig the next bit, Dan,' he handed him the spade.

'The ould dog for the hard road, as usual. I can't see too well but it looks like more stones. I think there's something else underneath them.'

He put the spade aside, and lowered a hand. 'I'm not sure what this is. Another root be the feel of it. But, a bit on the soft side, it's more like a piece of ould cloth. And what are all these small stones doing? Bloody hell, it is cloth. And it looks red. It couldn't be, it couldn't be, could it be me treasures?'

He knelt down so quickly, his cap fell into the hole. He stretched out both hands and felt underneath. 'We've found them, we've found them! And, imagine, only a foot away from where I'd searched before.'

He slowly pulled out the sodden package he had buried thirty years earlier. 'Me medals, me medals. Me poor decorations, I thought I'd never see you again. Be Jasus, the bastards never got you after all. Thank you, God!' clay fell off his trouser knees as he stood upright and offered his treasures to the heavens.

'And thank you too, me young conspirator,' he retrieved his cap. 'Without you and your plans, I'd have never found them. They'd have been lost forever. But, I wonder if they'll all be in one piece after so long underground? You carry them down and we'll open them in the house. Now, I know why you handed me the spade, you wanted me to find them. No flies on the Gunner. You're becoming a right rascal.'

Though it was summer, the package was heavy with damp. It was likely that moisture had penetrated the tins and saturated everything. The Gunner emerged with a saucepan of warm water as he was peeling off the first covering. 'You're like the fella unwrapping those Egyptian mummies. Now, give it to me. I tied it up, I should know how best to open it.'

Dan carefully uncovered the biscuit tin. The once-red lid was holed and rusted. 'Very thin, 'twas to be expected. But, look, the cape and the tablecloth did their work, it's much drier inside.'

He slowly unrolled the cloth and uncovered the embossed Queen Mary brass box. 'Just a bit dulled, didn't I do a great job? Now, for the nitty-gritty.'

After a few tugs, he lifted the lid and revealed the brown tobacco pouch. It seemed only slightly damp. He opened it up and inside was the paper which had protected his medals.

'Now, you strip that,' he handed him one roll. 'And I'll do the other one. Then we'll wipe the Vaseline off with that soapy water and we'll be in business.'

'You are like a hero returned from the wars,' he told the Gunner, as they sat on his favourite stone. 'Finally reunited with your old friends. Well done.'

Dan turned to Salvo who, head sideways, had been following operations from the flagstone. 'Extra helpings for you too tonight, me ould sego-tia. We'll enjoy a double celebration.'

The sun glinted off the newly uncovered sovereigns and the medals which Dan had pinned to his clay-stained shirt. The silver King George medal with its blue and white-bordered gold ribbon, whose reverse featured Saint George mounted on his horse. The rainbow-ribboned bronze Victory medal, whose central red strip mirrored Dan's shirt, and on whose reverse was inscribed 'The Great War for Civilisation 1914-1918'.

'Great to wear them again after all these years. And they're perfectly round, unlike the ones me visitors were left with. Look at those ribbons, buried so long and still with all their colours. And, I won't forget, 'tis thanks to you that I found them.'

'Dan, you are the one who twice earned them. Despite so many setbacks, you never gave up searching over all those years.'

'I took the advice of the travelling show acrobat. "Life's like a tightrope, if you stop you fall off."'

'We must always keep going. Now, we've only one little problem. How to tell your mother.'

'She has to find out some time, Dan. But, I am afraid she will be cross with me when she hears what we have been up to.'

'Don't worry, lave that to me,' the Gunner unpinned his trophies.

'I'll go up and see her and the Sergeant later on and explain everything.'

The evening Angelus rang out as if in celebration, as the boy kicked the dust on his way back up to the village. He had wondered how to finally reveal their secret to his parents, he was relieved the Gunner would do the job. As he approached the bridge, he saw his mother reading on the garden seat. There was no fooling her. 'I can see by your swagger that you are very pleased with yourself. Tell me what is going on,' she put down her book as he reached for the railings gate.

'The Gunner has some good news. What is the new novel about?'

'Never mind the book. I had a feeling you were up to some mischief down there, I hope he has not involved you in anything daft. He did not have you looking for treasure, did he?'

'He will come up later and tell you himself.' 'So, there were no drills for turnips?'

'It was others who said that, not me.'

'But you never said there were not. The poor Gunner, time his fortunes changed. We under-estimated him over the years, I believe he saved many lives in 1914. I did no baking today, go up to Mrs Delaney and get a few biscuits,' she handed him a shilling.

The Gunner arrived at seven, his cap at a new jaunty angle.

'Dan, you are looking twenty years younger,' his mother stood back from the door. 'We heard you had some news. Come in and tell us all about it.'

'I'm on the pig's back at last, 'tis a long story,' the Gunner put the tobacco pouch on the table and picked up a biscuit.

The boy's father looked across at his mother, as the Gunner revealed how he had been beaten up and his medals taken. But that they had been replicas, that he had earlier buried the originals in the rath. 'They've been hidden for thirty year and though I searched high and low for the last ten, I could never find them. That was 'til your son came along and narrowed the search area with his questions and maps. And this afternoon, after all our hard work, we found them. Here they are, you are the first in the village to see them.'

'Well, Dan,' his mother recovered from the shock. 'We can all take a lesson from this – and from your determination. I am sorry we never knew the full story. History in real life is less glamorous than in the books. You are a great man to have survived the ordeal – and your long silence. Your decorations were well-earned, you have done Toomevara proud. I am glad this fellow was a help. I'll forgive you both for keeping your search a secret.'

'I'm sorry mam, that was all my doing. If we hadn't kept it quiet, everyone in the village would have been nosing around up there. You should be very proud of this lad. But, he's not a lad anymore, he's a big man now. Well ready for his long trousers. And a clever one. Without him and his plans, me medals might have been lost forever.'

Dan reached into his jacket pocket. 'And, we've something for you too. Another bit of history we found.'

'Ireland's uncrowned king,' she examined the Parnell pipe. 'I will treasure this and put it on the mantelpiece with his medal next Ivy Day. You are a right pair of rascals keeping everything secret from me, but I suppose it was all in a good cause. I'll have to treat you both to a celebratory drink.'

The boy was taken aback, was his nationalistic mother mellowing?

'Hard to believe they were in the ground for so long,' his father held up the decorations. 'And three sovereigns, still shining like the day they were minted. There was treasure in the rath after all. You must have been very happy to see them again?'

'The best day of me life, Sergeant. Nearly as great as Armistice Day. I'll let Bill O'Meara, Mick FrenchShea and a few others see them, but I'm not sure what I'll do then. Lightning never strikes twice, they say, but I'd still be a bit anxious about having them below in the house.'

'Lightning will not strike twice as long as I am around, Dan. When you have shown them to your friends, just bring the medals to the barracks and I will lock them up for you. They will be safe there – and you can see them every fortnight, when you come to do your work.'

'I think you will be out on the town tonight, Dan,' his mother opened her purse. 'But, leave the sovereigns here and make sure your treasures are with you, when you leave FrenchShea's.'

'Thank you, mam, but you've a very bad mind! *Merci beaucoup* again for your biscuits, 'twas these very *Nice* which fuelled the start of our search.'

Soon everyone in the village had heard of the Gunner's discovery. Neighbours stopped him in the street to see the medals. People who had previously made fun of him now congratulated him. They marvelled that he had found his decorations after so many years.

'I don't think he'll be doing the hundred yards dash any more nights,' Paddy Dwyer told Gordon Birch.

'A wonderful story, I'll write a few words in *The Nenagh Guardian*,' correspondent Ned O'Donoghue took notes. 'We never appreciated all you had been through - and I heard you saved many lives during the war.'

Mrs Tierney called Dan into her drapery shop and gave him a new blue shirt. 'And here is a jacket and trousers that Pat never wore. You are both the same size, it will be a perfect fit.'

'You never lost it, Dan, none of us could ever keep up with you,' Big Jim O'Meara treated him to a pint in his Bridge House pub. 'If there was an election for mayor in the morning, you would win hands down. Now, have a seat, tell me the whole story and Minnie will make you a nice ham sandwich.'

The Gunner had become a celebrity, he was the proudest person in Toomevara. Children who had mocked him now followed in the wake of his pipe smoke. The PP and Doctor Murphy called down to examine the medals.

'This is to enhance the new image,' the doctor presented him with a shaving brush and mirror.

The heady days of revolution long forgotten, villagers laughed as they heard how he had tricked the gunmen. 'I understand you had a great harvest of turnips, leave it there,' Dick Casey's waistcoat hurling medals jingled as he shook the Gunner's hand. 'You never gave up, you're an example to the rest of us. You'll have a seat beside the wireless from now on for all the big games.'

'I'll be like the fella in the Goldsmith poem, Dick:

The broken soldier, kindly bade to stay,
Sate by his fire, and talked the night away;
Wept o'er his wounds, or, tales of sorrow
   done,
Shouldered his crutch, and shewed how
   fields were won.'

'But not while our man Phil Shanahan is on a solo from midfield,' Dick went out to serve Bill O'Meara.

'It is a terrible pity the sacrifices of Dan and men like him were not acknowledged earlier,' Bill paid for his newspaper. 'We should try and make it up to him in some way.'

'You never said a truer word,' the garage owner reached for his hat. 'I will go and have a word with Jim Hickey.'

George Powell met the Gunner in the village that evening. 'I'm going into Nenagh on Monday in the pony and trap, would you like to come for the day?'

Dan wore his new green jacket, blue shirt and dark trousers for the occasion. His lapel boasted a red rose from his garden. 'Howdy, pal, you're like a returned yank,' George opened the trap door for him.

'*Allons-y, chauffeur*! Let's go,' Dan made himself comfortable in the side seat. He recited John Masefield as their pony broke into a trot:

'It's good to be out on the road,
And going one knows not where...'

The trip took longer than usual. 'I never knew I'd so many friends,' Dan waved back to Mrs McLoughney and other villagers who saw him off from the barracks.

'It's like a royal procession,' George reined in the pony, as Paddy Horgan and his neighbours stopped them at the bottom of Lisatoggart.

The outing was a well-planned diversion. Jim Hickey and John Joe McCormack wanted Dan out of the way, while they whitewashed the house with a bucket of paint provided by shop-owner Tim Delaney. The day flew by as Peig Ryan and Eileen Searson scrubbed the tiled floor and varnished Dan's pieces of furniture. Gretta Cuddihy repainted the faded green door. The boy's mother brought down two freshly-washed blankets and a pillow for the Gunner's bed. 'What a pity we did not have time to fix the window,' John Joe wiped his hands, as they heard George Powell's trap turning down the road.

John Joe and his friends flanked the doorway, when Dan came through the hedge. He looked at their paint- flecked clothes. 'A guard of honour of artists, Millet's only in the ha'penny place. What's going on?'

'A little surprise,' Gretta laughed. 'Have a gander inside.'

'I'm in the wrong house,' the Gunner came out and went in again.

'It's like the Waldorf Astoria,' he looked from the newly-polished furniture to the red tiles and back again. 'Youse are an awful shower. When I recover from the shock, I'll borrow a gramophone and invite everyone down for a little hooley. It will be like the ould days at Ballinamona.'

'And here's something Mick FrenchShea handed in,' Jim Hickey gave him a note.

'Will you read it for me, Jim?'

Jim opened it out. 'Congratulations, Kitchener. We've lost your slate. Come up tomorrow night, some relatives home from America want to meet you.'

The following day, the Gunner gave the medals and sovereigns to the boy's father. 'A big help, Sergeant, thank you,' he watched them being locked away. 'I'll sleep soundly now, knowing that after all the waiting they're safe at last.'

11.

A New Mahogany Gramophone

*He was still smiling when Peig found
him in the morning*

'Go down and check on our hero and give him this little present,' his mother handed him two green mugs on Wednesday morning.

'And, do not squash it, some jam sponge to celebrate the new ware. And, maybe, soothe his vocal chords. We heard him leading the Frenchshea Choral Society with "The Wild Colonial Boy", when we were out walking last night.'

'Nothing wrong with a little sing-song,' the Gunner peered inside the bag.

'Nothing like a change of delph, either – and they match me porridge bowl. And, before I forget, I have some great tidings for you too.'

'What is the news, Dan?' he competed with Billy Delaney's whistling, as he returned the cows from milking.

'Be patient. Sit down there first on the stone and enjoy the sun, while I'll do the essentials,' he took his gifts inside.

'Are you sure you really want to hear the latest?' the Gunner finally emerged for the mugs' christening.

'Well, I'll brighten your day. I don't know where the year went, but your number one travelling show's coming back in a fortnight. They gave me posters last night to put up. You'll be able to enjoy their roundabouts and amusements again. I can't wait to hear their new dramatics and play clock golf around the square with comedian, Bert Patterson. And, maybe, share a drop of something strong in his caravan afterwards.'

'After the medals, that is the best holiday news yet, Dan. I cannot wait to get up in the swing boats again.'

Summer was the boy's favourite time of the year. Traveller Heaney arrived each June with a new selection of wire puzzles. The clinking of Dwan's lemonade bottles forecast precious pen-

146

nies carrying the new delivery into O'Meara's pub. The whirring of Dubliners' laden sports-cycles heading for Kerry brought faraway places closer. Gaily-scarved gypsies added to the excitement. While their horses grazed on the Pallas road riverbank, they skipped through the street shouting 'Soldering time, soldering time. Bring out your leaking kettles and saucepans.'

But the most welcome visitors were the travelling shows, with their conjurors, jugglers, and drama productions. And the swing boats in which, with a few tugs of the ropes, he soared like the swallows above Treacy's and the neighbouring houses. The Gunner was the first to meet the shows when they arrived each year. In return for organising their shopping and milk supplies, he was given free admission to every performance.

'You are right about summer, Dan. With holidays and the sun shining, it is the best time of the year. If I had my way, I would do away with all the other seasons.'

'Ah, will you hould on there?' the Gunner reached for his pipe.

'Don't they add spice to the year? Where would we be without Easter, Halloween, Christmas? All celebrated since time immemorial and every one a match for the one before it. Spring, when the rabbits pop out and you're up at carpenter Tommy

Barney's for a new spinning top. In autumn, you and your pals are flying sycamore seeds and collecting conkers and hazelnuts, while us elders bring home the turf and the harvest. Winter's not as bad as it's painted, either. You're able to slide the icy street at night in the shop window lights. And enjoy Heaney's puzzles and your reading indoors.

'Every season's a time to be cherished. And if it rains, I couldn't care less. Nothing like a shower to freshen up the countryside, and it's good to know that the sun is warming someone somewhere else. When I stand at the door of a morning, winter or summer, and the sun sweeps across the fields from Boland's mill, I'd nearly dance but for me leg. Those hills and plains draw me in, I feel I'm part of them too. Part of something bigger than meself. 'Twas all here before us, 'twill all be here when we're gone. Aren't we lucky to be able to enjoy such riches?'

'Dan, you would have made a great professor, you throw a new light on everything.'

'Some people feel sorry for me because I'm getting older,' the Gunner puffed until he was enveloped in smoke.

'But I didn't age inside. I stayed young, I lived, I enjoyed everything. That's the secret of life. Gone in a blink, it's a gift we've a responsibility to make the best of. And an equal obligation not to deprive others of theirs. Adding a few year is like opening the next chapter of one of your books or climbing a hill. The further you go, the more you discover. The easier it is to separate what's worthwhile from what's not. Nothing worth knowing can be taught. And something else you won't learn in school, the best things in life cost nothing. Did you ever hear of W.H. Davies? A hobo who became a poet, Bill taught me one of his verses:

> What little wealth true joy doth need!
> I pay for wants that make no show;
> I pay my way and nothing owe;
> I drink my ale, I smoke my weed,
> And take my time where'er I go.

'I might owe a few bob here and there but, even if the pension's gone, I can sit here day or night and admire the whole shebang, below and above me. What more could any millionaire do?

'From me grandstand seat, I watch the stars at play. What ships they've guided safely home, what stories they could tell. When the moon creeps over Keeper, I can smoke away and enjoy a world that most people seldom see. The swirling green and purple Auroa Borealis. Shooting stars which remind me of rapparee Galloping Hogan, racing through that valley at night with his booty. If I've learned anything in life, 'twas from neither books nor bible. Nature's been me teacher. And, as I said to Doctor Murphy the other day, the more content we'd all be if we were more in tune with what's around us.

' "Whatever about the chassis, there's nothing wrong with your mind, Dan," he looked over his specs. "Monarch of all you survey from your hilltop fort, the furze your golden crown. People try many things to survive. Prayer, booze, humour, the gee-gees. You may have found the best solution. A balanced life, in harmony with mother earth. Though I heard you were far from perfectly balanced leaving Harty's the other night..."

'The doc's a pro. You'll have clever pals like him too, as you progress. Make the best of your time. Enjoy the variety of life and, as Liverpool Pat preached, never let anyone get you down. And, before I fall off me own pulpit, stick at the books. I'm sorry I never learned to read properly, but I always kept me ears and eyes open, I learned as I went along. The war that damaged me also educated me. It taught me to see behind the words. To explore the things that mattered, not the fashions. And, never forget, a good deed's as easily done as a bad one. It's giving that rewards, help a few along your way. Now, Amen and be off with you.'

  ∾   ∾   ∾

Two mornings later, the Gunner staggered into the Garda barracks. 'Sergeant, the Huns, the Huns! They've finally got me. I saw them with me own two eyes. The gaz is coming down the hill.'

Guard Howard made the Gunner a cup of tea, while the Sergeant went down to investigate. The rath and the top of the hill were covered in morning mist, which the Gunner had mistaken for poison gas.

'Wear and tear, it is to be expected, Dan,' Dr Murphy called. 'You live life while the rest of us merely exist. I can get you into Nenagh hospital for a few days and have the doctors and nurses check you out. Even a Rolls does not survive to sixty-plus without a little attention.'

'The nurses would make a pleasant diversion, but I'd prefer to be in me own bright home,' the Gunner lay back in his freshly-painted chair. 'I'm just a bit weak. If the war didn't get me, nothing else will. I wonder if you'd ask the Sergeant to lave down the medals, they'd be the best company for me?'

'Stay in bed then for a few days and I will come to see you every morning,' the doctor put away his stethoscope. 'I will speak to the Sergeant about the medals. And get Peig Ryan to drop in and do your morning porridge and shopping, so you will not have to worry about food.'

'If she brought me a couple of bottles of stout and the latest news, that would be even better.'

'Consider it done, I'll write a prescription,' the doctor reached for his Parker.

The boy stopped at Harty's on his way to see the Gunner the following afternoon. 'Fig-rolls for Dan?' Jack refused his threepence. 'And here's a couple for yourself.'

Savouring his biscuits, he wondered how it was that shopkeepers, whom he had often thought to be mean, could also be generous. He would have to be careful not to be so judgemental. He turned into the now familiar Silver-mines road. Criss-crossed with hedges, the vast plain stretched in front of him to as far as the Gunner's favourite Keeper. It was like entering a green tunnel, as he walked between hedgerows laden with wildflowers which seemed to grow bigger every day. Birds cavorted and sang, he hoped Dan would be soon out to enjoy them all again. It was hard to believe it was only a fortnight since he had walked down here to commence the big search. So much had happened in such a short time. What a great adventure – and his holidays were only commencing.

As he approached the door, there was no sign of the familiar robin. Fit again, Salvo was probably back adventuring with his mates. But good news for the bird could be bad news for the Gunner who might miss him. He would wait until tomorrow before telling him. 'Some medicine for you,' he pushed the door open.

Wearing Mrs Tierney's new shirt, the Gunner was propped up on a white pillow, familiar red blankets dressed the iron bed. Peig Ryan had swept the floor and tidied everything. Dan's eyes had lost none of their keenness, but he was weaker than he had ever seen him before. 'Confined to barracks, your medicine's timely,' he opened the biscuits. 'I'm glad you're here. We've some things to talk about. Can you get down me medals, they're on the dresser.'

He handed them to the Gunner, everything the man had to show for his long life and his time in the war.

'Many memories in these,' Dan's right hand trembled, as he let the medals hang down from their brass pins.

'Like meself, a bit faded but we all survived. I'm slowing down now but I've no regrets. I always tried to do me best. In France with me mates, in the fields with Dick Hassett. The world doesn't owe us a living, you get out of life what you put into it. Doctor or labourer, the things you'll appreciate most are those you work for. Do them well, you'll always be able to look yourself in the eye.'

The Gunner lifted up the medals. 'Pin them on yourself and see what they're like.'

His shirt sagged, the decorations felt heavy. With some effort, the Gunner pushed himself up in the bed. 'I'll now enlist you as the first member of the Royal Toomevara Digging Platoon. All's well that ends well. I fooled me visitors and to-gether we soldiered in the rath until we found our treasure. Now, we must share me decorations. I've told the Sergeant that you are to have them when I'm gone. And that me ould friend Bill is to get the Angelus picture.'

'Thank you, Dan, I will mind them for you. But that will not be for a long time yet.'

'I hope not. But when they're yours, think of me sometimes. The work we did, the big adven-ture we shared. And how we even kept our secret from your mother. A sound woman too, always generous with her cakes – and she forgave us our roguery. I hope you both enjoy many books for years to come on your garden seat. And that she lets you back in the river soon to build more dams.

'Life flows like your river. If you've tricky times, remember Liverpool Pat's advice to go with the flow. Like me war, fighting changes nothing, only creates more trouble. The best things take time. I'd me ups and downs but I finally found the peace I'd dreamt of in no man's land. I met the Major, I found me medals. The people here came round in the end. Salvo got better. What more do I want?

'I was thinking of using those sovereigns to go back to France one day and pay me respects to me fallen comrades. I'll hardly do that now. But, it's an ill wind, I've had an even better idea. As I'm back in everyone's good books, when I'm better, I'll try and have a stone erected where those young policemen were killed. Dacent lads who'd served the village well and never harmed anyone. Charlie Healy from Cork and James Rocke, the breadwinner for his mother in Kiltormer.

'There's a shadow over Toome since. A little remembrance should lift it, restore the kindliness of the old days and make us proud of our village again. And it might help towards final recognition for me unfortunate friends, killed after they returned. Maybe that will be our next operation? Say nothing yet. It may require some ducking and diplomacy, though giving your mother that Parnell pipe might have lent us a head start. People here may be slow to change but they're as dacent as you'll find anywhere. They'll see eventually that remembrance is about respect and humanity, not politics. Now, stand to attention and give me a little salute.'

He put his feet together and lifted his right hand to his forehead.

'Well done, I can see you'd make a fine soldier,' Dan tried to reciprocate. 'But, learn from me own mistakes. Don't let anyone tell you yours is the greatest country on earth and send you off to kill for it. It's not. We're all the same down here under God's blue sky. Will you keep an eye on Salvo's saucer? And, one last thing. The hands aren't too steady. Could you get the penknife from the dresser and peel off a pipeful of baccy for me?'

'Did you ever think of getting a new pipe, Dan?'

'The oulder the pipe, the sweeter the smoke,' the Gunner chuckled hoarsely.

He cut off two thin strips, rolled them in his palm as he had seen Dan do so often and filled the bowl. 'Is that all right?' he handed him the yellowed half-pipe.

The Gunner pressed the tobacco a little further down with his thumb. 'Grand job, you're a great aide, the Major would be impressed. Would you pin the medals on me shirt, I'll wear them for a little while to remind me of the ould days. Now, take a biscuit for your walk home.'

The Gunner eased himself back on the bed, his head sank into the pillow. 'Are those me hands down there? I'm tired now and I don't want you to see me like this. But with Peig looking after me, I'll be ok again tomorrow, so make sure you come and visit me. And maybe you'll be able to walk me to the door to see me ould pals, the furze? Many a scratch the same fellas gave me, but they lifted me spirits every morning since I came back in nineteen and eighteen. But, to be on the safe side, not a word to the doc.'

'An aide's work is never done,' the boy stood to attention at the door. 'Do not worry, I will not tell the doc and I will keep an eye on Salvo until you are better.'

He dropped the door latch lightly. As he turned around, he heard a flurry of wings. Not one, but two redbreasts, started to chirp on the windowsill. Repaying kindness, Salvo had returned with a friend. The Gunner would not be alone. And, thanks to John Joe running out of time, he would be able to hear the birds through the broken window, just like Dick Casey's wireless.

The boy bit off half his fig-roll and scrunched the remainder into small pieces.

As he went to bed that night, he was happy that he had helped the Gunner. And that Dan had found his medals and finally gained the villagers' respect. He felt guilty about the times he had wondered if the decorations were there at all. But, persistence had paid off. He would never forget the rapture on the Gunner's face as he opened the rusted biscuit tin.

Nor the treasures he himself had discovered. The exhilaration of singular company, stirring tales of faraway places, a new appreciation of everything around him. His best teacher, the Gunner had endorsed the rightness of asking questions. Dan's courage matched his wisdom, he had demonstrated that all things were possible. He was looking forward to helping him on their next mission. But, how could he get around his mother this time? He knew a man who probably would.

Meantime, he could use his holidays to extend his cycle explorations. Was there anything to match the freedom of the bike? The dust flying from his tyres, the wind parting his hair as he sped down the hills. The Gunner had told his mother he was a big man now. It should be easy to persuade her to let him travel further afield, though he might not advertise how far. He had cycled all the leafy townlands from Clash to Cloncannon and the heights of the Devil's Bit. One day soon, he would pack a sandwich and ride to the Silvermines hills. He would stand on Keeper for the first time and admire the vista of five counties stretching all the way to the mighty Shannon. That would be a grand adventure, he thought, as the river lulled him to sleep.

Down in his house on the hill, the Gunner nodded off to the robins' serenade. He was smiling to himself. He dreamt that Jane O'Brien had returned from England and was nursing him. There was a lot to be said for being ill! Her dark hair swung, as she bent over the pillow and admired his medals. How happy he was that she could finally see them. Jane looked so fresh and beautiful, she had not aged like him and their other schoolmates. She put a record on a new mahogany gramophone and sat down beside him. It was his favourite song. He could hear the tramp of marching feet. His war was over. He was coming home at last to his favourite village. To a friendly welcome and to such a bright house. He could smell the fresh paint.

The Gunner was still smiling when Peig found him the following morning. His unsmoked pipe lay beside him. The slanting sunlight elevated St

George in rousing relief on his resurrected silver War Medal. Rainbow ribbons glowed, as the goddess Victory raced with flying robes on its bronze companion. Her palm branch raised aloft, arms outstretched, she welcomed a hero's final homecoming.

Acknowledgements

This novel is based on shell-shocked Gunner Dan Doherty, who enlivened my childhood village of Toomevara in pre-television days.

Hopefully it may lead towards long-overdue recognition for him, fellow-villager 'Old Mate' and other WW1 veterans, who were ostracised on their return from the horrors of Mons and Ypres. Over one hundred were murdered.

Thanks to Toomevara people who provided invaluable information: Ritchie Casey, Owen and Jackie Cuddihy, Lena Kilmartin, Bernie Leane of the Boland family, Colm Lynch, Father John Molloy, Hugh Maher, Donal Shanahan and Michael Tierney. Jane Bulfin, Local Studies, Tipperary Co Council Libraries, Helen O'Brien for her study of the Toomevara Clearances, Helen O'Toole, Hospital of Assumption, Thurles, where the Gunner died in October 1951.

Also to dedicated and helpful historian Tom Burnell – and Myles Dungan – for their books on the Irish in WW1, and to fellow-author John Sheehan. Intrepid manuscript readers Noel Lewis, Dympna O'Halloran, John McMahon, Frank and Pat McKenna, Peadar MacManais, Adrian Kenny, hard-pressed Senator David Norris and award-winning author Lissa Oliver. Other mainly polite advisors were Peter and Mary Costello, Mary Caulfield, John and Win O'Grady, and indefatigable *Sunday Independent* columnist, Liam Collins.

A special Thank You to Garry Cotter of the *Nenagh Guardian* and Ronan Dodd of the *Tipperary Star* for their consistent support. Provincial papers are the lifeblood of the community, long may they thrive.

Fran Carroll and staff of Dublin's National Library were generous with their time and expertise, as were Vanessa O'Loughlin, Writing.ie, Ken Clay, The Penniless Press, Charlie Payne of Charlies Medals Ltd, Andrea Cullen, Faith Coates and Andy Bambrick, Stephen Devlin, Events Manager, Hodges Figgis and the shop's Chief Buyer, Paul McGrath.

Thanks also to Karen Lynch and Hannah Burn – and another wonderful encourager, the late Marlene Lynch.

And old friends, Derek Ivory, Lauri Duffy, Brendan Gallagher, Gerry and John Flannery,

Acknowledgements

Pete Hogan, Shay and Von Lawless, Martin Mc-
Carthy, David Marshall, Val O'Donnell, Brendan
O'Reilly, Kieran Regan, ace photographer, Johnny
Bambury and Stephen of the Secret Book Store,
Dublin.

Salutations to friends who have sadly died:
David Marren, editor Pat Cunningham, journalist Kate Holmquist, Ulick O'Connor, Eileen
O'Meara-Walsh, Malachy Cardiff, Maxi McDon-
nell, the National Library's Gerry Lyne and Sir
Stirling Moss, who wrote Foreword for earlier
book.

Thanks to Anu Design team, Karen Carty
and Terry Foley, for their fine cover; author Lissa Oliver for her proofreading and layout. David
Givens of The Liffey Press for invaluable advice,
designer Susan Swaine and artist Bob O'Cathail
for his evocative linocuts. Also, Nielsen's Eleanor
Pigg, Heather Clark and Lucy Jung. Marie, Janice,
Kenneth and Dave at King's Printers. And Cap-
puccino maestro, Yari of Dunne and Crescenzi,
David and Paolo of Bar Italia and hard-working
Gary of Read's Print and Design.

A final big Thank You to long-suffering but
irrepressible Margie, who contributed generous-
ly towards production of this book – the Arts
Council of the Philippines. Apologies for any

omissions or errors, which I will happily correct in subsequent printings.

Please note, some names have been changed to protect people's identities. *Sláinte agus saol chugaibh go leir!*

Also by Brendan Lynch

Green Dust: Ireland's Unique Motor Racing History

Triumph of the Red Devil. Britain's First Motor Race – The Gordon Bennett Cup 1903

There Might be a Drop of Rain Yet: A Memoir

Parsons Bookshop: At the Heart of Bohemian Dublin, 1949-1989

Prodigals and Geniuses: The Writers and Artists of Dublin's Baggotonia

City of Writers: The Lives and Homes of Dublin Authors

Yesterday We Were in America: Alcock and Brown, First to Fly the Atlantic Non-stop

Princess of the Orient: A Romantic Odyssey